What the press says about Harlequin Romances…

"…clean, wholesome fiction…always with an upbeat, happy ending."
— *San Francisco Chronicle*

"…a work of art."
— *The Globe & Mail*, Toronto

"Nothing quite like it has happened since *Gone With the Wind*…"
— *Los Angeles Times*

"…among the top ten…"
— *International Herald-Tribune*, Paris

"Women have come to trust these clean, easy-to-read love stories about contemporary people, set in exciting foreign places."
— *Best Sellers*, New York

OTHER
Harlequin Romances
by ROSEMARY POLLOCK

Many of these titles are available at your local bookseller
or through the Harlequin Reader Service.

For a free catalogue listing all available Harlequin Romances,
send your name and address to:

HARLEQUIN READER SERVICE,
M.P.O. Box 707, Niagara Falls, N.Y. 14302
Canadian address: Stratford, Ontario, Canada N5A 6W4

or use order coupon at back of book.

Summer
Comes Slowly

by

ROSEMARY POLLOCK

Harlequin Books

TORONTO • LONDON • NEW YORK • AMSTERDAM • SYDNEY • WINNIPEG

Original hardcover edition published in 1976
by Mills & Boon Limited

ISBN 0-373-02067-8

Harlequin edition published May 1977

Printed in U.S.A.

CHAPTER ONE

'YOUNG woman, in case you're having difficulty with your hearing, I'd better repeat that I have no intention of tolerating any sea views.'

The diminutive Maltese girl who had come over from behind her flower-banked reception desk to try and sort out the considerable problem which seemed to have arisen began to look a little desperate.

'But, Mr Debenham . . .'

'I've heard enough "buts". My granddaughter explained my requirements when she got in touch with you from London.' Robert Debenham, internationally celebrated author and nightmare of hoteliers from New York to Singapore, glanced up balefully at a slim, auburn-haired girl who had been smiling apologetically at the receptionist. 'If you didn't make my requirements clear, Susanna, you're a bigger fool than the rest of them put together.'

Susanna Baird looked rueful. She was used to this kind of scene and she was used to getting the rough edge of her grandfather's tongue, but that didn't make the situation any easier to handle. 'I did explain, Grandpapa, but perhaps——'

'Then what's the matter with this place?' The powerful voice with the just-perceptible Scots accent boomed out across the vastness of the Grand Hotel Melita's green and white foyer like the rumble of an approaching earthquake, and the Very Important Guest's hard

5

blue eyes were once again turned on the unfortunate receptionist. 'My granddaughter's as dim-witted as any other woman, but she's not a liar. She told you I'd need a suite, and she told you it would have to be well out of sight of that revolting stretch of muddy water out there. So——'

'Mr Debenham ...' The Maltese girl looked appealingly from the enormous figure stretched out in a wide moss-green armchair to the attractive female relative standing beside him, and then she gave a little shrug of helplessness. 'I don't know who accepted the reservation, but all our suites look out on the sea.' She added nervously: 'It's a beautiful view. Most people like——'

'Most people like a number of things that I find repellent. Where's the manager?'

'The manager is not here, sir.'

'Then I'll go to another hotel. Susanna, get a taxi.'

'Wait ... Just one moment, Mr Debenham.' The receptionist's eyes had lighted on a masculine figure just emerging from the lift, and something in her face suggested that she felt like a swimmer on the point of drowning who has been unexpectedly washed up on the beach. She darted over to intercept the man, who was walking towards the main entrance, and as he stopped and swung round she poured forth a torrent of rapid Maltese. Susanna, watching with detached interest, decided that he was anything but pleased at being held up, and she felt a touch of curiosity about his exact position in the hotel. He certainly didn't look like a member of the staff—with his beautifully cut light grey suit and his general air of distinction, he seemed a good deal more like one of the Melita's wealthier and more valued patrons. On the other hand, the receptionist obviously regarded him as someone to whom it was possible to turn in a crisis, and although just at the moment he looked bored and a little impatient, he was undoubtedly paying attention. After a few seconds he glanced at his watch and with an air of resignation accompanied the girl back to where Robert Debenham was still sprawled with a kind of arrogant placidity in the massive armchair.

'Good evening, Mr Debenham.' His voice was light and fairly pleasant, but there was a clipped, cool precision about it that somehow made his Maltese accent seem very noticeable, although his English was good. 'I am so sorry that this confusion should have arisen. Obviously a member of my staff has been extremely careless. Every suite we have overlooks the sea, and your reservation should not have been accepted. However,' glancing at his watch again, 'if you will agree to have dinner here, as my guest, we shall do our best to find you alternative accommodation ... Of course, it will have to be at another hotel.'

Robert Debenham shrugged expansively. 'My dear fellow, as long as it's out of sight of your overrated coast, I don't care where it is.'

Watching the other man, Susanna thought she saw his rather thin lips tighten, but he bowed slightly and managed something in the nature of a flickering smile.

'And you will have dinner with me?' For the first time he lifted his dark eyes to Susanna, and it seemed to her that they grew bleaker than ever—which, she thought, was saying something. 'You too, of course, Miss ...?' He hesitated.

'Baird,' supplied the figure in the armchair, 'Susanna Baird. She's my granddaughter and general factotum. If I could run to it I'd naturally make an effort to preserve my sanity by employing a male secretary, but I can't pay the exorbitant rates demanded by establishments like yours and still afford luxuries.' As he spoke he glanced up at the girl beside him with something approaching a diabolical gleam in his eyes, and she smiled resignedly. Since he could easily have afforded a dozen secretaries—male or female—she had often thought it was a pity he didn't engage one, but there were certain rather peculiar jokes which he was in the habit of repeating with the regularity of clockwork, and this was one of them. Now he was watching the expressionless face of the Maltese with the same sort of unholy amusement. 'We'll both be delighted to have dinner with you,' he said handsomely. 'I am right in assuming that you own this place?'

'Yes.' The other man bowed again, but this time it was a barely perceptible inclination of the head. 'I am Ramiro St Vincent de Säez.'

'Well, I'm very happy to have made your acquaintance, and so's my granddaughter—aren't you, Susanna?'

Again Susanna merely smiled. It struck her all at once that the man in front of them was really quite strikingly good-looking. His looks were not of a type that particularly appealed to her, but she supposed a lot of women would probably find him devastating. His well-trimmed hair was very black and inclined to

8

wave, and his regular features had an almost feminine beauty about them—although there was nothing feminine in the strength of the rather noticeable chin, or the uncompromising firmness of the mouth. His eyelashes were long for a man's, and the oddly lustrous dark brown eyes beneath them could have been shatteringly attractive—if it hadn't been for a shuttered coldness in their depths that actually made Susanna want to shudder. She didn't know whether it sprang from dislike and resentment of herself and her grandfather, or from something deeper and more permanent, but ridiculous as it was that look seemed to chill something inside her.

Despite the almost youthful quality of his looks, she decided he must be somewhere about forty, and she found herself wondering casually whether he had a wife, and if so whether they would be meeting her at dinner. It was somehow rather difficult to imagine him with a wife.

'I will see you in an hour's time,' he was saying. 'That is, at eight o'clock. In the meantime, you will probably wish to rest—perhaps to change—and I will give instructions that our best available rooms are to be placed at your disposal.' He turned and spoke to the young receptionist, still hovering nervously beside him, and she hurried away. 'When Josephine returns,' he went on, 'you must describe to her your precise requirements. She will do everything necessary to arrange your accommodation elsewhere.'

When he had left them, and his elegant figure—tall by Maltese standards—was moving rapidly away across the burnished mosaic of the floor, Robert Debenham chuckled.

'That's an interesting character,' he said suddenly, 'I daresay I'll put him in my book. What did you think of him?'

'I think he's—not very nice,' Susanna said truthfully, and startled herself. She didn't often pass unflattering judgments on anyone until she had had an opportunity to find out a good deal about them.

'Do you, now? Well, well!' He chuckled again. 'We'll know more about him when we've had dinner with him.'

When her grandfather had been whisked away in the lift to take temporary possession of the most luxurious suite the Hotel Melita had to offer, Susanna had the necessary brief consultation with Josephine, the head receptionist—the trouble Josephine was being put to made her feel uncomfortable, but she could at least console herself with the reflection that it was hardly her fault—and then, just as she was moving away from the desk, something touched her arm and she turned round to find herself face to face with a startlingly glamorous girl.

'I hope you'll excuse me.' The newcomer's voice was husky. 'You'll think I've a real nerve—talking to you like this, I mean. It's just that I couldn't help noticing you're with Mr Debenham, and—well, I'd say I've read just about everything he's written. I come from Sydney and it's fantastic that I should meet up with him like this.'

Accustomed to dealing with fans—sometimes in large numbers—Susanna smiled with a touch of amusement. 'That's very nice of you. Mr Debenham always likes to hear that his books are appreciated.'

'Well, they're appreciated by me.' The girl had long, gleaming ash-blonde hair that looked natural, and besides being made up with a skill that suggested she might be a model, she really was astonishingly pretty. She was wearing a lavender blue trouser suit that bore the unmistakable stamp of Rome, and everything about her had a subtly expensive look. Not for the first time it struck Susanna that some of the most surprising people took an interest in the literary output of Robert Debenham. 'I was wondering ...' The attractive voice was just a little hesitant. 'I was wondering whether your employer might give me his autograph.'

'I'm sure he would,' said Susanna. She added a little drily: 'He's not my employer, though. He's my grandfather.'

'Well! Aren't you lucky?' Judging by the starry expression in the other girl's candid brown eyes she was quite serious, and Susanna's amusement grew.

'You're an admirer,' she remarked.

'Yes, I am. He's such a brilliant writer. He must know a lot about people.'

'Oh, yes ... he knows a lot about people. Shall I get his autograph for you, or would you like to ask him yourself?'

'Could I?' The eyes grew bigger and starrier than ever. 'I'd love to speak to him.'

'Well, we'll be having dinner here tonight. If you are, too, I'll bring him over to you.' Her grandfather could always be relied upon to be charming to a fan.

'But that's fantastic! Thank you so much! You're

having dinner with the Marquis, aren't you?'

'The Marquis?' Susanna echoed.

'The Marquis St Vincent de Säez, the owner of this hotel. Oh, I know I shouldn't have been listening, but I couldn't help overhearing your conversation. He's quite something, isn't he?'

'I suppose so. If you like that type.'

The Australian girl lowered her voice conspiratorially. 'All the girls on the staff are mad about him.'

'Are they? Well, I daresay he's got a wife to protect him.'

'That's just it, he hasn't. He's a widower. He was married to this beautiful French girl who got killed in an air crash, and the maid who does my room says that ever since then he hasn't even liked women.'

So that was it! That look in his face, particularly noticeable when his eyes rested on her, Susanna, hadn't just been a figment of her imagination. It had puzzled her, and being interested in people she liked to get to the bottom of things like that. Suddenly she glanced at the large ormolu clock facing her across the width of the foyer, and saw that it was nearly half-past seven. She'd have to get away before the other girl embarked on further revelations.

'Well, I'll see you later ...' She stopped. 'I don't know your name, do I?'

'Oh, I'm Jackie ... Jackie Wilverton. And thanks,' she said again, 'thanks a *million*!'

As she made her way up in the lift, Susanna decided that this stay in Malta might be going to be rather entertaining.

CHAPTER TWO

IT didn't take her long to have a bath and change, and by the time it was five minutes to eight she was completely ready. But she knew that her grandfather was unlikely to have been hurrying himself, and before leaving the room allotted to her by Josephine she paused for a moment in front of the huge dressing-table mirror and studied her own reflection rather thoughtfully.

Susanna was twenty-three years old and she was attractive. Her skin had the magnolia-pale clarity that goes with red hair, and there was a neatness about her features that tended to give her the look of a Dresden figurine. Her nose was small and straight, and the arch of her slender eyebrows had never yet called for the assistance of a pencil. But her eyes were her most distinctive feature. Large, fringed by thick brown lashes, they were as blue as the Mediterranean, so despised by her grandfather, had been when they flew over it that afternoon.

But so far her looks had made very little difference to her life. Apart from one or two boy-friends in whom she had felt no particular interest, she didn't take much notice of men, and she had become quite skilled in the art of keeping them at bay when, as they frequently did, they took too much notice of her. Never in her life had she been even slightly in love, and lately she had begun to wonder whether she would ever be. Marriage, after all, was still supposed to be the ultimate aim and object of most normal young women, especially those not really interested in the idea of a career—and unless being responsible for her grandfather could be said to be a career in itself, Susanna had no particular occupation. But sometimes, recently, she had had a feeling that she might never marry. Somehow she couldn't imagine it; she couldn't see herself as anybody's wife.

After frowning critically at her reflection, she switched off the lights in the big, comfortable bedroom, and hurried along the quiet corridor outside to rap on her grandfather's door.

A few minutes later, as they were being wafted silently downwards in the green-carpeted spaciousness of the lift, she told him about Jackie Wilverton.

'She's young and glamorous, and she'll give your ego an enormous boost, so be nice to her, won't you?'

'I'm invariably nice to attractive young ladies who like my books. Did she tell you whether she had a favourite?'

'No. I just gathered she thinks every word you write should be printed in gold.'

Robert Debenham smiled complacently. 'Delightful girl.' He looked at his granddaughter, and one of his eyebrows ascended quizzically. 'You're looking attractive tonight. I'd better keep an eye on this de Säez chap.'

Her eyes twinkled. 'That won't be necessary, he's not interested in women.' She added: 'But he's a real live Maltese marquis, so you can have a lovely time pumping him about his distant ancestors. Your book should be off to a flying start.'

'H'mm, well, if he helps me to get the feel of my

subject, it may be.' Suddenly he grinned almost boyishly. 'And Susanna, don't worry, I feel sweet-tempered tonight. I'll be as mild as a lamb.'

In the foyer they were met by an anxiously helpful Josephine, who told them that the Marquis was waiting for them in a cocktail bar known as the Saracen Room. She escorted them to the door personally, and a few seconds later they discovered their host. He was standing in front of a magnificent many-coloured mural depicting life in a mediaeval Arab village, and he was talking to one of the barmen. In a dinner-jacket he seemed even more good-looking, but as he came towards them the smile on his lips never touched his eyes, and watching him Susanna found herself wondering whether his presence among the guests could really be very much of an asset to the running of his hotel. Whether or not she imagined the hostility that seemed to lurk behind the bleak brown eyes, he managed to convey the impression that he would much rather have the place to himself, and as he escorted them to a corner table she saw his cool glance rove disparagingly over the patrons of his establishment.

He drew out a chair for Susanna, and then one for her grandfather. 'I hope you have been comfortable,' he said. 'I understand that arrangements have been made for you to be accommodated at the Hotel Medina. It's a very fine hotel in the centre of the Island. You will not be troubled by the Mediterranean there, I assure you.'

'Excellent!' Robert Debenham was definitely feeling expansive. 'Though I must say this place of yours

15

appeals to me. If it weren't for the outlook from your windows——'

'Of course, I understand.' The Marquis changed the subject pointedly, and as they started to discuss Robert Debenham's reasons for visiting Malta, Susanna sat back in her chair. Now her grandfather would be in his element.

'So far,' he was explaining, 'every one of my novels has had a modern setting. But I'm beginning to feel the urge to go back a bit ... to try and work out what life was like for the men and women who lived at some more absorbing period of history than the present.' He leaned back, studying his whisky glass through half-closed eyes. 'I'm getting too old to be obsessed with the present.'

'One does not need to be old, Mr Debenham, to be tired of the present.' There was a strange amount of feeling in the Marquis's quiet voice.

'No.' The other man looked at him shrewdly for a moment and then resumed the study of his glass. 'But a writer can get the feeling, especially when he's young, that it's up to him to deal only with the world as he knows it ... with his particular bit of time, and the places and people he's familiar with. Leave the past to Dickens and Tolstoy and the Brontës, and concentrate on recording the twentieth century. He wants to get to grips with reality, and he thinks reality is the present.'

'And you feel that it is not?' Again that note of quiet intensity.

'Of course it's not. Reality is the whole saga of human experience from the Creation up to the present day, and what happened this morning is not necessarily any more interesting or important than what happened six thousand years ago. It's all one big tapestry, and a novelist should work on whichever part of it catches his imagination.' He stopped abruptly and chuckled. 'I'm getting on to my hobby-horse. In a minute or two my granddaughter will start taking disciplinary action.'

The Marquis glanced at Susanna briefly, as if neither her approval nor her disapproval could be of the slightest importance. 'But I am deeply interested in what you say.' She noticed that his voice, coloured for the first time by some sort of enthusiasm, was really very attractive. 'I have often felt . . .' He hesitated, as if trying to find the right words. 'I have often felt that there can be a kind of—solace in becoming absorbed in the past, if, perhaps, one is not satisfied with the present.'

'Mmm.' For a few moments, Robert Debenham subjected his host to a penetrating blue stare. 'You mean it can be a relief to pretend that the present doesn't even exist, or that the past is more important. I think . . .' a tiny, reflective frown appeared on his wide forehead, 'I'd say that's rather a dangerous idea. It's probably just as well to live your own life here and now.'

'Possibly.' A barely perceptible shrug. 'But you were talking about your book.'

'Yes, I was, wasn't I?' He seemed to be collecting his thoughts. 'Well now, the thing that's got my imagination going at the moment is a certain bit of Maltese history . . .'

The two men talked for a long time, and Susanna,

quite used to sitting on the sidelines, amused herself by studying her surroundings. The Saracen Room, obviously designed to commemorate the Moslem occupation of Malta in a way likely to appeal to the Island's visitors, was an inspired creation, and she wondered whether the Melita's proprietor ever took any interest in the planning of such things. The walls were lined with glowing murals telling the story of the Arabs' life on Malta, and everything in the room had been carefully chosen to fit the general theme. Wall-lamps in the form of flaring torches threw a subdued light on to a mosaic floor scattered with leopard-skin rugs, and around the antique brass-topped tables more conventional types of seating accommodation mingled with a selection of camel saddles and colourful piled-up cushions. Later, when they moved into the big main dining-room, they encountered a contrast, but Susanna was more impressed than ever. For although this was the epitome of formal luxury it still managed to be original—not simply a carbon copy of any dining-room in any top hotel. The midnight blue carpet, flowing under Moorish arches into every nook and cranny of a vast circular room, gave her the feeling of being afloat on a southern ocean—she hoped it wouldn't affect her grandfather in the same way—and clusters of pale pink roses adorning each damask-covered table enchanted her.

Although she couldn't have said exactly why, she was beginning to have an idea that she might find the whole of Malta enchanting.

Her grandfather and the Marquis were discussing the great Turkish siege of the sixteenth century, and

18

her grandfather was explaining why it absorbed him as a background for a novel.

'It seems to have been almost the first time your people emerged as a people,' he told his host. 'And I find them fascinating. I know the Knights of St John were running things, but I'm not interested in them. My *dramatis personae* will be almost entirely Maltese.'

'We are a race of mongrels.' There was an unexpected tinge of dry humour in the Marquis's voice. 'Phoenicians, Carthaginians, Greeks, Romans, Normans, Arabs, Turks, Italians, Spanish, French ... even British.' He smiled faintly. 'They all came here, and they all became a part of us. Some more than others, of course.'

Robert Debenham's eyes began to twinkle. 'From the Arabs, for instance, you adopted an extremely sensible attitude to women. Keep 'em out of sight, and make sure they toe the line.'

'That attitude has disappeared now. Women in Malta are as free as they are anywhere else.' His voice was almost sombre, and Susanna couldn't resist putting a word in.

'You sound regretful,' she said.

He looked at her. 'I think modern life is not ideal for your sex, Miss Baird.'

'You mean we're too independent?'

'I mean your values have become distorted. You have been exposed to corruption.'

Susanna blinked. 'Isn't that putting it a bit strongly?'

But at that moment they were interrupted, for Jackie Wilverton had just entered the dining-room, and once she realised that her hero had already arrived she

19

obviously made up her mind to advance upon him without any further delay. She was wearing a turquoise evening dress that made her look as pretty and as wholesome as a Gainsborough painting, and when she came to a halt beside their table, Robert Debenham glanced up with immediate interest. Now that she was actually face to face with the literary lion himself some of her courage seemed to desert her, and she flushed and hesitated, but Susanna quickly came to her rescue.

'This is Miss Wilverton, Grandpapa. She's a terrific admirer of your books.'

'My dear ...' Exuding urbanity, her grandfather stood up. 'This is a very great pleasure.'

'Well, it certainly is a pleasure for me, Mr Debenham.' Jackie Wilverton's confusion was beginning to evaporate like mist in the warmth of the famous author's affability, and as she looked up at him her smile was devastating. 'I think you're just about the greatest writer——'

'That's very charming of you.' He beamed at her, and turned to indicate his host, who had also risen. 'I don't know if you've met the Marquis St Vincent de Säez, who is lucky enough to own this splendid hotel.'

Susanna's lips twitched, and she glanced at the Marquis. To her surprise he was staring at Jackie Wilverton with what definitely looked like interest, and—could it be her imagination, or was there a gleam of appreciation in his eyes? Whether there was or not, he moved quickly to pull forward an extra chair, and if Jackie had by any chance been reluctant to join the party, it looked as if one way and another she might have found it difficult to escape.

As it was she seemed overwhelmed, and the attractive shyness that a few moments earlier had been beginning to recede swept over her again, apparently robbing her of speech. Whether it was the cool dark gaze of the Marquis or merely the close proximity of Robert Debenham that was responsible, Susanna couldn't quite decide, but she suspected it was a mixture of both. Sitting between the two men she resembled a glamorous but self-conscious schoolgirl, and the ageing Scotsman whose work she admired so ardently threw himself with enthusiasm into the task of being charming to her. He certainly wasn't accustomed to having dinner in the company of every fan who demanded an autograph, but it had been his host's idea that she should join them. Her rapt interest was flattering.

The next hour went by pleasantly—or at least both Robert Debenham and Jackie seemed to think so, and their host seemed to relax a little. But just after nine o'clock, to Susanna's surprise, her grandfather made a move to break the party up. She herself didn't feel any urge to drag the evening out, for none of her fellow-diners had paid any particular attention to her and although she was used to playing second fiddle to her grandfather, she wasn't used to being quite so totally ignored. But, on the other hand, she had barely finished her icecream and the host hadn't yet had a chance to ask whether anyone wanted coffee. Temperamental her grandfather might be, but this wasn't like him.

And then she realised he was apologising. 'These damned air journeys are more tiring than you think

'... I feel as if I've been hit by a sledgehammer. Susanna——'

He had been leaning against the table—rather heavily, she noticed. Then suddenly, without warning, he fell back into his seat. Something was obviously wrong, and Susanna made an instinctive movement towards him, but even before she was out of her chair the Marquis de Säez had beckoned to a passing waiter, and was giving instructions for a doctor to be called.

'Grandpapa!' Desperately anxious, Susanna bent over the big figure now slumped alarmingly in the plush-covered chair, and put an arm round him. 'Grandpapa...'

His eyes were closed, but his colour was normal—in fact he looked normal in almost every respect. And then, as Susanna interposed herself between him and the onlookers by leaning forward to study him more closely, he suddenly opened both eyes—and almost immediately closed one of them again in a quite unmistakable wink. But after that he started to make what looked like desperate efforts to sit up, and the Marquis, putting Susanna aside very much as if she were an unnecessary piece of furniture, stepped forward and took the situation in hand. Not only did he successfully help the patient—who now seemed to be fully conscious—into what looked like a comfortable sitting position, but with one small gesture of his hand he ensured that all those fellow-diners who had crowded forward for a closer look were tactfully induced by members of his staff to return to their seats, so that within less than a minute the only onlooker left, apart from Susanna, was a white-faced and trembling Jackie Wilverton.

Jackie's eyes were wide with fright, and she kept repeating the same words over and over again. 'But this is terrible! What's the matter with him? It's just terrible!'

'Grandpapa ... are you all right?' Once again, from the distance to which she had been forcibly removed, Susanna attempted to speak to her relative, and was rewarded promptly by a faintly quizzical smile. But Ramiro de Säez, bending almost solicitously over the older man, assured him positively that there was no need whatsoever for him to talk, and even looked round at Susanna with a gleam of annoyance in his dark eyes.

'Miss Baird, I suggest that you go and wait in one of the lounges.' His voice was a little impatient. Then his glance shifted to include Jackie, and he added, 'Take Miss Wilverton with you.' His tone softened a little. 'This has been a shock for her. She should have some brandy, I think.'

Susanna stared at him. 'I'm not going anywhere,' she began, and then was startled and at the same time tremendously relieved to hear her grandfather's voice.

'Do as you're told, Susanna.'

'All right ... all right, Grandpapa.' She swallowed, feeling her lips dry with anxiety. It was ridiculous and dreadful that she should be sent away like this, but whatever happened she mustn't argue with him. If only she understood what was happening! Why had he winked at her like that? Had it been a wink?

She spoke in an undertone to the Marquis. 'Please, as soon as possible I'd like to speak to the doctor.'

He bowed. 'Of course.' Then he beckoned to one of the girls from the reception desk who had come in from the hall to hover anxiously nearby, and as he said something to her she nodded and turned to smile reassuringly at the two female guests.

'Would you like to come with me?'

At that time of the evening most of the guests were either out touring the night-spots of the Island or still lingering over a late dinner in the restaurant, so the big, softly-lit lounges were quiet and almost empty. The chairs were deep and comfortable and the colour-scheme soothing, and Susanna had to admit to herself that once she and Jackie Wilverton had been comfortably installed in a secluded corner behind a protective screen of palms and oleanders, she felt better. A few minutes later a waiter appeared bearing not one but two glasses of brandy—possibly the Marquis had decided after all that Jackie might not be the only one in need of a restorative—and the Australian girl, who was still very upset, sipped gratefully at the glowing liquid.

But Susanna left hers untouched. She wanted news of her grandfather, and after a very few minutes she began to feel very restive. At first it had been rather a relief to be whisked away, but when ten minutes elapsed, and then fifteen, and then twenty, and still there was no word from the dining-room and no sign of anyone coming to speak to her, she began to feel as if she might be in the grip of an unpleasant dream.

'I should think,' said Jackie suddenly, 'they're getting him to bed. They wouldn't move him to that other hotel, not tonight.' Helped by the brandy, she was rapidly becoming her old confident self again, and

24

Susanna, who usually took considerable pride in her own cool head and her ability to keep control of a situation, found her an oddly reassuring companion. She herself had been thinking in terms of her grandfather's being moved to hospital, and at the thought that it just possibly might not be necessary, she relaxed—very slightly. But only slightly, and by the time two soberly clad masculine figures emerged from behind the potted palms and began to bear down on her she had succeeded in working herself into such a state of tension that she actually jumped.

And the realisation that one of the figures was none other than the Marquis St Vincent de Säez himself did nothing whatsoever to calm her down.

But the other man, who was obviously the doctor, looked relaxed and cheerful, and as she looked into his face a surge of relief swept over her.

'Miss Baird?' He held out a hand to her. 'No, no, sit still ... sit still.' His face was round and paternal, and his dark eyes were kindly. 'My name is Manduca. I was called to attend your grandfather.'

'And how is he?' Her soft voice was husky.

'There is nothing wrong with him—nothing at all. Except ...' the doctor shrugged slightly, 'he has perhaps been working too hard. Of course he is not a young man, and it may be that he needs a rest. It is a case of sudden exhaustion. The journey from England will have brought it to ... to ...'

'To a head?' suggested Susanna, smiling with relief.

'Of course, to a head.' The doctor beamed back at her. 'But there is no need to worry. He is here for a holiday?'

25

'Not really. He came to work on a book.'

'But here in Malta it is easy to rest, and there will be many opportunities. You will look after him, I am sure.'

'I will,' Susanna promised. Then she added: 'Where is he? Can I see him now?'

'Yes, yes, whenever you like. He is upstairs in my good friend Ramiro's best suite, and for tonight he will stay there.' The bright brown eyes twinkled sideways at the Marquis, and Susanna found time to experience a sensation of mild shock. Could anyone honestly think of a man like that as 'my good friend Ramiro'?

Soon afterwards the doctor left, and while de Säez was escorting him to the hotel's main entrance Susanna said goodnight to a relieved Jackie Wilverton and slipped upstairs in the lift. It was in the 'best suite' that her grandfather had changed for dinner so she had no difficulty in finding her way to it, and when for the second time that evening she rapped lightly on the bedroom door, she was rewarded by the sound of his own voice, calling to her to come in.

He was in bed, but so effectively propped up against a mass of snowy pillows that he was virtually sitting upright, and he was certainly looking very much himself.

'So there you are.' He gave her a curious look. 'Did you see de Säez?'

'Yes, I saw him. And the doctor.' She moved to the foot of the bed, and smiled at him a little anxiously. 'How are you, Grandpapa?'

From under their hooded lids his blue eyes gleamed at her. 'Never felt better in my life.'

'But you're tired. You're going to have to rest a bit and enjoy life more. You gave us all quite a fright down there——'

An explosive sound like a strangled chuckle interrupted her, and the invalid's lips began to twitch. 'You weren't taken in by that?'

'Taken in?' she asked blankly.

'Well, you don't suppose I really passed out, do you? That dinner wasn't the best I've ever tasted, but the fillet steak was quite edible, and on the whole the strawberry gâteau didn't go down too badly either. I was rather looking forward to sampling the coffee, but my dramatic sense told me it might be best to stage my performance a little before the formal conclusion of the meal.'

'Your ... performance?'

'Yes, my gullible child, my performance. Well, you might show more appreciation of my theatrical talents.' She was staring at him in a way that he obviously found irritating. 'Don't stand there looking as if half your wits have taken a holiday!'

She looked incredulous. 'You don't mean to say you weren't unwell at all?'

He nodded cheerfully. 'Of course that's what I mean to say!'

'And you only pretended to be unconscious?'

'Yes, I only pretended. It's disgraceful, isn't it? But I had a reason, Sue. I always have a reason!'

'I don't believe it! You're only saying all this so that I shan't worry about you.'

He looked amused. 'Well, you can think that if you like, my dear, but I don't know what I've ever done to

27

give you the idea that I might be getting considerate in my declining years. What did the local quack tell you?'

'He said he thought you needed a rest.'

Her grandfather chuckled with obvious relish, and eased himself into a more comfortable position. 'Well, short of suggesting the whole thing was a put-up job that's about all he could say. I could see he was a puzzled man, but naturally it didn't occur to him that such a solidly respectable character as myself would be "swinging the lead", as I believe the expression is.'

Susanna sank weakly into a chair. 'But why . . .?'

'Why? Now there's a question.' His eyelids drooped again. 'You'll find some *marrons glacés* on the dressing-table. Take one yourself and then pass them over, will you?'

Automatically she obeyed, though without taking advantage of the invitation to help herself, and Robert Debenham accepted the box of expensive confectionery with gratification.

'Nothing quite like *marrons glacés*. Thought that ever since I was a boy.' He became aware of the fact that his granddaughter was still standing beside the bed, and he looked up. 'What's the matter?'

She drew an exasperated breath. 'Grandpapa, I asked you *why*.'

'Why what?'

'You know very well what!'

He put the *marrons glacés* aside and smiled up at her amiably. 'Why did I decide to become an invalid? I felt like cadging some hospitality, and this seemed the most sensible way of setting about it.'

She frowned in bewilderment. 'What do you mean?'

28

'Simply that our friend de Säez interests me. I wanted an opportunity to study him and his household at close quarters, so I tried a small gamble which happened to pay off.'

'Gamble?' Susanna blinked her long eyelashes. She was beginning to feel she must be rather stupid.

'Well, you could call it that. I had a hunch that this particular scion of the Maltese nobility might, despite appearances, be equipped with a fine sense of the fitness of things. I didn't think he'd allow an—er—ageing celebrity like myself to be laid low in an hotel while his own house could be made available, and it turned out that I was right.'

'What do you mean?' Susanna repeated foolishly, feeling an apprehensive chill spread through her.

'Just that we're going to stay with him, Sue,' her grandfather smiled complacently. 'Both of us. For an unlimited period. So stop looking as if you're going to pass out on the spot, and start working out what you're going to say when you thank him!'

CHAPTER THREE

SOON after eleven the following morning Susanna found herself standing for a few moments in the cool shadow of Kingsgate, the huge, square, cream-coloured archway that dominates the main entrance to the old city of Valletta. She had done a lot of walking that morning, and although it was only April the sun was hot—or so it seemed to her. She had stopped to give something to a frail little elderly nun who was collecting for the poor orphans of the Island, and as she fumbled in her purse for a suitable donation she was glad she had an excuse for lingering, just for a second or so, in the shade. Before long, she knew, she would have to be getting back to the hotel, for at three o'clock that afternoon she and her grandfather were to be collected by the Marquis's chauffeur and whisked away to begin their sojourn in the Marquis's house. But this morning she had felt the need to get away by herself for a time, and as her grandfather was to be in bed until lunchtime she was more or less free to do what she liked.

So she had taken a taxi into the heart of Valletta, and having been set down near the ancient Palace of the Grand Masters had set out to absorb some impressions. Although she was tempted to do so, she didn't go into the Palace, or into any of the museums and historic buildings that surrounded her—they would have to wait for an occasion when she had more time at her disposal—but instead she just wandered about the beautiful old city, taking in something of its unique atmosphere, and finding herself unexpectedly captivated by everything about it.

Kingsway, the long, gently sloping main thoroughfare, was lined for most of its length with bright, enticing shops in which it seemed to be possible to purchase anything from French cosmetics and English paperback novels to Libyan silk and locally made silver filigree jewellery, and she spent a lot of time simply window-gazing. But if the shops were fascinating, it was the vivid cosmopolitan crowds thronging the wide

30

road—which was closed to traffic—that really intrigued Susanna. There were a good many tourists about, and most of the countries of Europe seemed to be represented, not to mention America and the Far East. Everyone was relaxed and in a holiday mood, and it struck her that the Island's tourist industry seemed very well organised. Fleetingly, once again, she had thought of the Marquis de Säez. He obviously secured an important part of the tourist industry, and she found herself wondering just how much work he actually put into the business of catering for the visitors. Quite a lot, probably, for she had received a strong impression that he was a man who liked to work. But, remembering the look of distaste with which he had favoured the guests in his cocktail bar the night before, she found it difficult to believe that he enjoyed associating with them.

Valletta, she discovered, was a peninsula town, bounded on three sides by the Mediterranean, and every now and then, gazing down dark and narrow side streets, she had caught a glimpse of the jewel-bright sea. The side streets themselves, often steeply sloping and sometimes actually formed from hundreds of stone steps, were mysterious and fascinating beyond anything she had expected, for half-hidden in the shadows were beautiful old doorways that had once belonged to the fine houses of the merchants, and here and there the windows were protected by exquisite iron grilles. Magnificent antique lanterns hung from the walls, and in the dimness behind some of the windows caged canaries sang.

It was Shakespeare's Verona—imprisoned for ever,

31

with all its romance and enchantment, on a warm little southern island.

But beyond Kingsgate the picture was different. As soon as the ancient maze of streets had been left behind, mediaeval Verona disappeared like a mirage, and as Susanna stood beneath the gate all the colour and noise of modern Malta surged around her. Bright red and white buses and shining sports cars roared past her in the sunlight, and feeling a little bewildered she moved to the edge of the kerb, hoping to be able to stop a taxi. But the road at that point was very wide, and the confused mass of traffic, swirling round a huge central roundabout dominated by fountains, reminded her of Paris. There didn't seem to be a taxi in sight.

And then, out of nowhere, a large silver-grey car appeared beside her. Almost noiselessly it drew to a halt, and with an odd sort of sinking sensation in the pit of her stomach she recognised the driver. It was the Marquis de Säez.

'Good morning.'

One of his well-manicured hands was resting lightly on the steering wheel, and as he glanced up at her she felt there was a suggestion of disapproval in his face.

'May I give you a lift?'

She hesitated. Under ordinary circumstances she would probably have said no, for there was nothing about this Maltese nobleman that inspired her with a desire for his company. But there certainly didn't seem to be many taxis about, she wasn't familiar with the bus service, and there wasn't much doubt that if she decided to be independent it would be quite a while before she managed to find her way back to the hotel, which would drive her grandfather into a frenzy.

'Thank you,' she said, and smiled at the Marquis. 'Actually I'd be very grateful. I'm on my way back to your hotel.'

With a slight bow but with no lightening of his expression, he climbed out of the driving seat and moved round to hold a door open for her. Sighing with relief, she sank back against the cool dove-grey upholstery of the front passenger seat, and as he got in beside her she glanced at him.

'This is very lucky for me. I'd had just about as much as I could take for one morning.'

He let in the clutch, and they edged their way out into the noisy mainstream of traffic.

'You react badly to heat?' It sounded more like an accusation than a question.

'Well—no, actually I don't.' For a moment she had felt tempted to laugh, but laughter in the presence of Ramiro St Vincent de Säez seemed out of place, so she restrained herself. 'I'm used to heat,' she told him, 'Grandpapa and I travel all over the world, and we spend quite a lot of time in hot countries. Only two months ago we were in Singapore, and before Christmas we had several weeks in Tanzania. You see,' she added, as if so much globe-trotting called for some sort of explanation, 'Grandpapa was looking for ideas.'

'But now he has an idea.'

'Oh, yes, he's very excited about Malta.' Turning her head, she caught a brief glimpse of the world famous Grand Harbour, blue and cream and lovely in the sunlight. 'I'm excited too,' she confessed suddenly.

The Marquis ignored this. 'Your grandfather,' he

remarked forcefully, 'has to rest now?'

'Yes, of course. Oh, I'll see that he rests.' She smiled almost confidingly at the man beside her. 'You know, he really does listen to me sometimes.' As she spoke, she remembered that both she and her grandfather were soon going to be indebted to Ramiro de Säez for quite a lot of hospitality, and at the thought of the shameless piece of deception being perpetrated by her relative her cheeks turned pink. Her grandfather really was the absolute limit! But, on the other hand, his little scheme wasn't doing anybody any harm—his prospective host was probably looking forward to his company—and in any case, she couldn't give him away.

Rather uncomfortably she began, 'I should have said before that we're both—Grandpapa and I—we're really very grateful to you for——'

De Säez interrupted her. 'Please don't be grateful to me, Miss Baird. I have a great respect for your grandfather—not merely for what he has achieved, but for what he is. He is essentially strong and positive. He knows what he wants from life, and I have no doubt that he usually gets it. In addition he has, of course, a very fine mind, and it will be a great pleasure to me to be able to talk to him at length. As for yourself ...' The momentary enthusiasm which had lent his voice colour and softness died away. 'I hope you will not be bored in my house. There is much to see in Malta, and one of my cars will always be at your disposal. Do you drive?'

'Yes, I do. I love driving.'

'Then you had better use the small Lotus. It should

not be too heavy for you. I will let you have the keys, and you can go where you like.'

She stared at him. 'That's very nice of you, but I do have to spend quite a lot of time with my grandfather. He dictates at least twenty letters every day, and I have to type them. And there are other things—he's always wanting me for something or other ...'

'Just the same, it would probably be better for him if he did not see too much of you during the next few weeks. He needs to rest, and you, no doubt, would remind him of work.'

'But ... but I——'

'You can amuse yourself, can't you?'

The car had turned into the forecourt of the Grand Hotel Melita, and before she had had a chance to think of anything to say they had to come to a halt before the main entrance. A commissionaire hurried down the steps to open her door for her.

'Until this afternoon, Miss Baird.' Ramiro de Säez was getting out of the car, and rather limply Susanna did the same. Across the shining bonnet he looked at her, coolly. 'You feel insulted.' His voice was very quiet. 'Think a little more of your grandfather—and perhaps a little less of yourself?'

Without another word he slipped back behind the steering wheel, and the Jaguar's engine purred into life again. To Susanna's fury it was more than a minute before she realised that she was still standing exactly where he had left her, staring foolishly after the sleek grey shape of his car.

CHAPTER FOUR

THE road leading to the Casa de Säez was a road that
ran steadily inland, winding its way among the low,
rocky hills—green in winter, brown in summer—that
lie at the heart of Malta. It started out as a good road,
broad, well made and neatly lined with officially
planted oleander bushes, but it wasn't long before it
began to deteriorate, and as Susanna and her grandfather, piloted by the Marquis's chauffeur, started
their climb into the hills it soon narrowed itself down
to little more than a rough track.

The chauffeur, Emmanuel, had turned out to be a
cheerful countryman with the physical appearance of a
mediaeval Turk and a command of colloquial English
which betrayed the fact that he had served for ten years
in the Royal Navy, and he was a mine of information.
He told his passengers that they had arrived in Malta
at the very best time of the whole year, and they would
never see it looking more beautiful. Using one large
brown hand to guide the Jaguar around a series of
bumps and pot-holes which he would obviously have
been able to negotiate blindfold, he kept the other free
for the occasional sweeping gesture with which he
pointed out items of interest, and every so often, evidently feeling that some particular point could not be
emphasised properly with his back turned to the
visitors, he took his eyes right off the road and swung
round to face them.

Happily, nerves had never been one of Robert
Debenham's problems, and he bore the more hair-

raising aspects of the journey with the tranquillity of a sleepy Siamese cat. Susanna experienced a few more qualms, especially when, on a bend, they missed an oncoming donkey cart by what looked like a quarter of an inch, but she was too captivated by everything she saw to have much time for feeling frightened, and every time they reached the summit of a hill and a new panorama opened itself out before them, she turned to her grandfather with a little gasp of delight.

The hillsides were vividly green, for the winter, apparently, had been very wet, but the lower ground and most of the fields were carpeted with the vivid crimson of giant clover, something she had never seen before. To the Maltese, Emmanuel told her, the clover was known as *silla*, and he also told her that before another week had gone by it would be cut for use as animal fodder. Whole families would work together on the harvesting of it, for in its way it was a valuable crop, and when it was cut it would be loaded into donkey carts and carried away for storage in barns.

'In Malta,' said Emmanuel, 'we harvest everything. It's a hard life for our farmers.' He concentrated for a moment on the road. 'My father, he was a farmer. It's a tough life, uh?' But even as he uttered the words his tanned face broke once again into its irrepressible smile, and the smile seemed to say that however tough life might be for some, the Almighty undoubtedly knew what He was doing. Which meant that there was nothing whatsoever to worry about, and with all its shortcomings, the world really was a wonderful place in which to live.

After about half an hour they came to the top of a

long, steep hill, and as the car slipped between the tall stone piers of an ancient gateway, they reached their destination. The rough rutted track that formed the only road leading up to the gate had yielded suddenly to the smooth tarmac of a private driveway, and all at once they were moving forward through a dense thicket of trees and shrubs. Gnarled old carob trees, slender firs and silver-grey olives were jumbled together with such abandon that Susanna was reminded of a primaeval forest, and as they slowly glided on beneath the spreading branches—which met overhead to form a grey-green roof—the warmth and brilliance of the April afternoon were so effectively shut out that she began to find the tangle of growth almost unnerving.

Her grandfather's thoughts were evidently running in the same direction.

'Dear me!' he murmured. 'The Ogre's Castle! Never tell me, Sue, that I don't lead you into interesting adventures.'

She made a face at him. 'It may,' she remarked softly, 'turn out to be more interesting than you bargain for.'

He chuckled. 'Impossible,' he assured her. 'I have the highest hopes of this—ah! Ahem!' He stopped, and bent his large head to peer through the window. 'The dwelling itself, I take it.'

They had rounded a bend in the drive, and directly in front of them there loomed a massive stone house, in the form of a tower. It was obviously very old, and the passage of the centuries had left its honey-coloured, bougainvillaea-clad walls with a look of having grown out of the hard, rocky hill-top to which they clung. Its windows were square, deep-set and unevenly placed; and those on the ground floor, Susanna noticed, were heavily barred. But it stood well clear of the trees, full in the golden light of the sun, and the neat square forecourt in which the car was just coming to rest was bright with budding oleanders and the purple splendour of morning glory.

Susanna's eyes widened. It was the most romantic-looking place she had ever seen in her life. To think of such a house being wasted on Ramiro St Vincent de Säez!

With good-humoured care Emmanuel helped her grandfather to extricate himself from the rear seat of the Jaguar, and then he moved over to the heavy iron-bound front door and pressed an unseen bell. Almost immediately the summons was answered, and a plump, dark-haired woman in an ageless black dress appeared on the threshold. She smiled at Emmanuel, and they embarked on a short conversation in Maltese, at the end of which the chauffeur beckoned encouragingly to his English charges. Susanna, who had lingered to admire the morning glory, hurried forward, and the woman smiled again, this time in her direction.

Emmanuel gestured vaguely. 'There is no one home this afternoon, uh? But this is Carmen ... she will look after you. She has a lot of English.'

The woman nodded several times, apparently in confirmation of this statement, and at that moment Robert Debenham, who had taken his time about strolling over, appeared behind his granddaughter.

Carmen eyed him benevolently, and her toothy smile widened.

'Hello,' she said.

'Hello!' the large figure exuded urbanity, and Susanna recognised at once that her grandfather's association with the Casa de Säez had started off well. He had discovered an ally.

The Marquis, it seemed, did not live quite alone, for he had an aunt, the Signurina de Säez, who shared the Casa with him and at this hour of the day would normally have been in her room. But on this particular afternoon the Signurina had been forced to pay a visit to a distant relative who lived on the other side of the island, and as the Marquis had business to attend to there was no one but Carmen on hand to welcome the English guests. She did her job very adequately, and it wasn't long before Susanna and her grandfather were each installed, complete with luggage, in their respective rooms, but Emmanuel's statement that she had 'a lot' of English had been rather an exaggeration, and despite her overflowing affability, communication with her was tricky.

Visitors passing through the main door of the Casa de Säez came first into a large, white-walled entrance hall, and as they crossed the threshold the first impression most of them received was one of almost monastic simplicity. The hall was flagged—unusual, Susanna was to realise later, on an island where most floors were tiled—and there wasn't a rug in sight. Several magnificent antique chests were ranged against the walls, and the glorious patina on the old wood bore witness to loving and continual care. But apart from a beautiful oriental lamp, which was suspended from the centre of the beamed ceiling, and which caught her eye as it swung gently in the breeze from the open door, there was nothing decorative in evidence anywhere. A chill ran through her, very like the chill she had been conscious of when the Jaguar had first plunged into the shadow of the wood, and without going any further, she knew that something vital was absent from the house. It had no heart.

But the wide stone stairway that led upwards through round white arches to the bedrooms was light and airy, and the warm breeze fluttering curtains at the scattered windows brought with it a faint scent of flowers. The scent seemed to hover in the atmosphere on the upper floors of the house, and everywhere there was a sense of coolness and space. And when Susanna saw the bedroom that had been allotted to her she stood still on the threshold, astonished and enchanted. Even here, she recognised, there was an air of restraint about the decor ... but at the same time it was one of the most attractive rooms she had ever seen. Walls, ceiling, and the mosquito net suspended above the bed were white, dazzlingly white, but the predominating colour was green—green silk bedspread, green taffeta skirts hanging from the pretty antique dressing-table, green and cream rugs scattered about the polished wooden floor. Recessed in an archway, two large, square windows had been opened wide to admit the brightness of the afternoon, and a small, comfortable-looking armchair, upholstered in green and piled high with cushions, had been pulled invitingly close to them. From the ceiling hung a pretty little gilded lamp, a smaller, more delicate version of the one Susanna had noticed in the hall below, and the mirror on the dressing-table had an unusually lovely silver frame. It was a room that someone had furnished with care.

Her grandfather announced that he intended to take a short rest—by which, as she knew, he meant that he wanted to read for a while, and be free to absorb the feel of his new surroundings in peace. He declined Carmen's offer of tea—a beverage which she obviously believed most British people were ready to absorb at any time—and showed no marked interest in any of the other refreshments suggested to him, but Susanna said gratefully that she would love a cup of tea, and when she was at last left alone she settled down in the chair by the window to wait for it. The last two days had been hectic and worrying, and she wanted to relax. Here, in this quiet green room, it shouldn't be difficult.

Resting her arms on the sill, she leant forward to look out of one of the windows ... and immediately received a second delightful surprise. For just below, nestling close to the old stone wall of the house, was a fairy-tale garden. Probably as old, in parts, as the building itself, it had obviously been the work of many generations, and gazing down at its lush, sleepy beauty, Susanna decided that it was undoubtedly enchanted. Surrounded on all sides by walls and shaded by ancient olives and cypresses, it was a place in which time itself might be expected to stand still. Between the graceful shapes of the trees, flowers ran riot. Pink and white oleanders, giant Madonna lilies, roses, the scarlet flame of the hibiscus ... Susanna loved gardens, and the excitement of discovering this one made her breath catch in her throat. Even the encompassing walls were ablaze and alive with colour, for plumbago and honeysuckle, bougainvillaea and morning glory jostled each other with such wild abandon that the old grey stone beneath hardly had a chance to show itself. And there were other things, too, in the garden. Little stone figures, faun-like and mysterious, peeping at one another through the leaves ... Somewhere, the bubble and whisper of a fountain throwing water into a pool.

There was a knock on the door, and Carmen came in, bearing a tray of tea. The tray was attractively laid, and the tea, it turned out, excellent. But Susanna didn't waste a great deal of time over it, for there was only one thing she wanted to do just then, and that was to find her way down to the enchanted garden below. It drew her—almost as if, from somewhere among the silver-grey leaves of the olive trees, a voice had called to her.

It didn't take her long to find her way down to the hall, and as she stood hesitating, wondering whether or not to make her way out through the front door, she caught sight of a narrow passageway leading off to the right. At the end of the passage there was a door which stood slightly ajar, and glimpsing through the narrow crack a ribbon of blue sky, she realised that it led into the open. There didn't seem to be much doubt that it would lead into the garden.

Less than a minute later she was on the other side of the door, standing on a wide stone terrace. Sunlight fell all about her, warm and caressing, and the

43

air was heavy with the haunting, confused scent that she had first noticed inside the house, and the peace and stillness exuded by old stones. Just below, spread out in front of her like a living fairy tale, was the garden.

Six broad, shallow steps led down to it from the terrace, and she moved quickly towards them, impatient to find out for herself what it felt like to stand beneath the whispering olive trees. Where did all the paths lead, she wondered ... and where was the unseen fountain? But just as she reached the head of the steps something touched her; something cool and moist pressed itself against her ankle, and she turned to find a large dog standing behind her.

Susanna adored dogs, and this was one of the most beautiful specimens she had ever seen in her life. Tall and very graceful, it was the colour of ripe corn, and its brown eyes held a look of almost human gentleness and benevolence. Its head was very handsome, with large prick ears and a slender, elegant muzzle, and it struck her at once that she had never seen anything quite like it before. It belonged to no breed she had ever encountered.

She held out a hand to it, and it sniffed her fingers with care. The long, slim tail began to move approvingly, and she felt accepted.

'Now, who do you belong to?' she wondered softly. 'Not the wicked Marquis, surely? I don't believe it, you're too nice.'

The dog sniffed her hand again, and then moved on down the steps. With an odd sense of embarking on an adventure, she followed, and letting the animal lead

44

the way she found herself, after a minute or two, in a tiny orange grove. The trees were heavy with unpicked fruit and she was tempted to stop and examine them, for she had seen oranges grown in other parts of the world, and she knew quite a lot about them. But the large dog was still moving onwards, and besides, the sound of rushing water was much louder now. Somewhere, just around the corner, there was something quite fascinating—she was sure of that.

Seconds later, she found it. Tucked away in the heart of the garden, behind the orange grove, sun-warmed and secluded, there was a tiny open space. In the middle of the open space there was a goldfish pond. And in the middle of the pond, on a jagged, natural rock, there sat a little stone cherub with the most be-guilingly jovial expression she had ever seen on a statue. Clutched tightly in its chubby arms was an up-turned jar; and from this jar sparkling water perpetu-ally cascaded into the pool below. Susanna was enchanted—almost as enchanted as she had been when she first saw the garden. She looked around for the dog who had mysteriously led her to the spot, and in the same instant made the discovery that she was not alone in that quiet place.

On the other side of the pool, close to the edge, a little boy was squatting on the ground. He could, she decided, be about seven years old, but he was rather thin, and she had a feeling he was undersized for his age. He was a good-looking little boy—not unlike a delicately carved stone figure himself—and if his night-dark hair and eyes were anything to go by he was undoubtedly Maltese. Not, of course, that that was surprising. The dog who had accompanied her from the terrace had gone over to him and was sniffing him all over with a kind of eager, anxious affection, and she saw now that another almost identical dog was lying nearby.

The boy was looking straight at her, with the grave uneasy eyes of a small wild deer, and she smiled at him.

'Hello.'

'Hello.'

Moving round the pool, she sank down herself on to the sun-warmed ground, and wondered how much English he would be likely to understand.

'What's your name?' she asked.

He edged away a little. 'My name is Minu.' The childish voice was very clear and clipped, and he didn't seem to have much of an accent.

'Well, that's a nice name. Do you know. it's the very first time I ever met anyone called Minu?'

'Is it?' He looked at her with a little less suspicion. After a moment's obvious hesitation, he said: 'It isn't my real name. And my father doesn't like it. He says it's silly.'

'What's your real name, then?'

'Lorenzo.' Half apologetically, he added: 'My father says *that's* a proper name.'

An intriguing thought entered Susanna's head, and she wondered why it hadn't occurred to her before.

'Who is your father, Minu?' she asked.

He looked surprised. 'My father is the Marquis,' he said solemnly, 'the Marquis Ramiro St Vincent de

Säez.' He repeated the names slowly and carefully, like a lesson.

Susanna felt shaken. So the Monster—as she had named him in her imagination—had a son! Since he had, after all, once been married, there was no reason why he shouldn't have children, but somehow the possibility had never occurred to her. She looked at Minu with real sympathy. No need to wonder why the unfortunate child had such an uncertain, apprehensive air about him. He didn't look strong, either, and probably needed a lot more care and attention than he was likely to receive. She realised that she could be doing the Marquis a serious injustice—it was, of course, quite possible that he was devoted to Minu—but at the same time something told her that if she thought that she would be deluding herself. There was nothing about Ramiro de Säez to indicate that he would even be able to tolerate the presence of a child in the house. Quite suddenly another thought struck her.

'You haven't any brothers or sisters, have you?' she asked Minu.

He shook his small dark head. 'No.' Thoughtfully, he added : 'I'm glad I haven't.'

'I expect you have lots of friends, anyway,' Susanna suggested bracingly.

Wriggling slightly, he turned away from her, and began to concentrate all his attention on a large goldfish which had risen to the surface of the pool. 'Well,' he said after a pause, 'I've got Simba and Julian.' As he spoke, the dog beside him pricked up its ears and emitted a small sound. He put an arm round it, and it dawned on Susanna that Simba and Julian were the names of the dogs.

'But haven't you any other friends?' she persisted. She was beginning to feel there was something wrong, something strange and unnatural, about the way in which this child was being brought up, and although it was no concern of hers she felt an urge to find out more. She looked at Minu, who had made another small wriggling movement but hadn't answered her question, and tried another tack. 'Don't you go to school, Minu?'

'No, I don't have to go to school. Brother Bernard comes to teach me things.'

'Who is Brother Bernard?'

'He's a monk. He's very nice, and I like him. I don't want to go to school, and I don't want to have any friends—only Simba and Julian, and Brother Bernard.' His voice trembled suspiciously, and he took a tighter hold on the golden dog.

Susanna felt annoyed with her own clumsiness, and she set out instantly to repair the damage. 'I think you're very lucky,' she assured him gently. 'I wish I had friends like Simba and Julian.'

He looked round at her slowly. The threat of tears receded, and the dark eyes grew curious. 'Who are you?' he wanted to know.

She smiled at him. 'I'm Susanna. I'm staying here with my grandfather.'

A look of interest flashed across his face, but whether or not the information pleased him she didn't have a chance to find out, for at that moment a voice was heard calling 'Minu!' and the small figure beside her jumped. Susanna stood up.

'Minu! Minu!' It was a woman's voice, rather high-pitched, and it conveyed a mixture of anxiety and irritation. Seconds later its owner came into sight, and as she hurried towards them through the orange grove Susanna recognised immediately that she was about to come face to face—sooner than she had expected—with the Signurina de Säez, the Marquis's aunt.

The Signurina, who looked as if she might be somewhere in her fifties, was thin and rather tall, and seemed in a state of nervous agitation. She was wearing a very well-cut but absolutely plain dark blue dress —which wouldn't have suited her under any circumstances—and her black hair, which looked as if it might once have been beautiful, was drawn tightly back from her face into an old-fashioned knot. There wasn't much about her that could have been expected to impress a stranger, and on the whole she looked rather forbidding.

Yet, sizing her up swiftly, Susanna experienced a sudden feeling of sympathy for the older woman. Spinsterish and unimaginative she probably was, and it seemed fairly obvious that she didn't even know how to make a child like her—one glance at Minu's face was enough to indicate that—but her anxiety and relief at finding him were transparently genuine, and it was difficult to doubt that she was fond of him. It seemed to Susanna that she was probably a timorous person, far more likely to be oppressed herself than to oppress another human being, and instinctively the English girl knew that whoever it was who was making a mess of Minu's young life, it couldn't be this nervous middle-aged woman.

Smiling apologetically, Susanna took a step forward, and the Signurina stopped dead in her tracks.

'You are Miss Baird?' Her accent was much heavier than her nephew's, and the sight of the English guest seemed to frighten her a little.

'Yes, that's right. You're the Signurina de Säez, aren't you?'

'Yes.' The dark eyes dropped. 'My nephew told me about you. Your grandfather also. I hope you are comfortable.'

'Thank you, we couldn't be more comfortable.' Earnestly, Susanna hoped that in speaking for her grandfather, she wasn't tempting providence. She glanced down at Minu, who was still squatting on the ground. 'I hope your nephew's little boy isn't late for anything. If he is, it's my fault. He's been talking to me.'

'Oh ... don't worry. It doesn't matter.' The Signurina looked vaguely and uncertainly at Minu. 'Come inside now, *haninh*. It's time for your bath.'

With a look of resentment, Minu began to get up. The operation took him some time, and at first, as he dragged himself slowly and rather awkwardly to his feet, Susanna imagined he was dawdling deliberately, in order to annoy his aunt. But when he suddenly slipped back on to his knees, and was forced to begin the process all over again, it suddenly dawned on her that there was something actually wrong with one of the child's insubstantial legs. And when, a few seconds later, he did finally succeed in standing up, she saw

50

quite clearly what the trouble was. His right ankle was seriously deformed, and the foot attached to it so twisted that to all intents and purposes he must be a cripple.

Instinctively, she turned to the Signurina de Säez, to find that the older woman was watching her with a look on her face which could have been fear.

'It was an accident.' Even her voice was taut and defensive. Obviously Minu's handicap was something she found it hard to talk about.

'I see.' Susanna wanted very much to know more, to ask how it had happened, and when ... and whether there was thought to be any possibility of treatment. But she knew she mustn't say more in front of the child, and in any case it didn't seem likely that the Signurina would be communicative on the subject. So she simply smiled at Minu.

'Well ... goodnight. Sleep well. Perhaps I'll see you in the morning.'

'I have to do lessons in the morning.'

'Later on, then?'

'Yes. Perhaps.' He smiled back at her—a small, polite, grown-up smile. 'Goodnight.' And without waiting for his aunt he began to limp away through the orange grove, in the direction of the house.

The Marquis's aunt stood still for a moment, her eyes on the ground.

'We have dinner at eight o'clock, Miss Baird. If there is anything you need——'

'Thanks, I'm sure there won't be anything.' She hesitated. Rather shyly, she added: 'Please call me Susanna.'

'Very well ... if you wish.' A thin, half gratified smile touched the Signurina's face. Then awkwardly, abruptly, as if unable to think of anything more to say, she turned and hurried after the limping child.

CHAPTER FIVE

AT twenty minutes to eight that evening Susanna found her way to her grandfather's room, and rapped lightly on the door. After a moment's silence she heard his voice instructing her to come in—and to her relief the voice sounded relaxed and good-humoured.

Going inside, she closed the door behind her and looked round the room with approval. It was a long room—much bigger than her own—and dark beams cut across the whiteness of the ceiling. There was a lot of dull gold about the furnishings ... curtains, rugs, lampshades, the heavy, elaborate counterpane on the old Spanish bed, and even a beautiful Russian icon on the wall above the bed all reflected the same colour. Like her own room, it was essentially peaceful. But it had also, she noticed, been equipped to meet the requirements of a busy writer, for near one of the windows a handsome modern desk had been installed, and on it there stood a powerful Anglepoise lamp.

Robert Debenham, attired in a dinner-jacket, was reclining in a large armchair which like the desk had been placed near one of the windows, and to her satisfaction he looked even more relaxed than he sounded. As she came towards him he glanced up, and the life of

Mozart which he might or might not have been reading was put aside.

'Still in one piece, Sue?' His face was quite serious, but his eyes gleamed. 'It struck me that the Ogre might keep a few lions around here somewhere, and with true misogynist's zeal might have thought of throwing you to them.'

'I don't suppose he'd hesitate for an instant.' She subsided on to a stool beside him, and shook back her gleaming hair. 'But although I've looked round quite a bit I haven't found any lions ... so far.' She smiled mysteriously, and added: 'I found something else, though.'

'Ah!' The life of Mozart was tossed on to a table, and a look of enjoyment appeared on his cherubic face. But for nearly a minute Susanna said nothing more, and he became impatient. 'Well?' he prompted, as she still said nothing. 'Well? What have you found? The bleached bones of his victims?'

Her eyes grew serious. 'I found his family,' she said quietly, and she told her grandfather about Minu.

When she had finished he didn't speak immediately, and then he looked at her thoughtfully. 'Are you suggesting de Säez ill-treats this brat?' he wanted to know.

'I couldn't say, Grandpapa.' She sighed, and began to rock herself backwards and forwards, clasping her knees. 'But that poor little kid is unhappy, I do know that. If you ask him anything about himself he looks like bursting into tears. Besides, he's more or less a cripple, and I'm certain something could be done for that foot of his—I'm sure in a case like that an operation would do the trick.'

'M'mm. Mention it to his father, then.'

'His father! His father and I are hardly on speaking terms.'

Robert Debenham looked amused. 'Well, if the description you gave me of your last conversation with our host was at all accurate, I can see that relations between you could be somewhat strained for a while. But there may be the odd moment—just now and then—when you're not actually at one another's throats, and when that sort of moment arises, you'll just have to seize the bull by the horns and rush straight in with some well-thought-out advice.' He grimaced slightly. 'What an appalling mixture of metaphors! I need a rest badly.'

Susanna eyed him reproachfully. 'I believe you're hoping for trouble!'

'Oh, no, not I!' Smiling beatifically, he leaned back in his chair. 'De Säez would be bound to get the worst of it in the end—there's no future in quarrelling with a woman—and, personally, I like the chap. The extent to which he has my interests at heart is quite touching.' His smile widened. 'I gather he feels I stand in need of protection ... mainly, of course, from you, my heartless, dominating granddaughter.'

Susanna laughed. 'You're quite shameless! If he only knew what an unspeakable trick you're playing on him——'

'What trick? My health is in an extremely fragile state.'

She sobered instantly, looking into his face. 'Grandpapa ...'

He glanced at his watch, still smiling. 'Yes?'

54

'There isn't anything wrong, is there? I mean—you were telling me the truth last night?'

'The absolute truth.' Suddenly he turned his piercing blue eyes on her. 'Heavens above, child, you're not worried about me, are you?'

'No, of course not.' Knowing perfectly well that he loathed gestures of affection, she nevertheless bent and kissed the top of his head. 'I'm going down now. Follow me after a minute or two, won't you? It would be awful to be late.'

'Would it?' He had repossessed himself of the life of Mozart, and looked as if he might be planning to settle down for the evening. As his granddaughter reached the door he called after her.

'What about the woman? She's a scarecrow, I suppose?'

Susanna turned, one hand on the door-handle. 'Well, no ... not exactly. She isn't young, of course, and she isn't glamorous, but I should think she'd improve quite a lot if just occasionally someone were kind to her.'

'I don't feel like being kind.'

'Nonsense, you know you'll be charming to her.'

She left him at last, and went downstairs into the cool dimness of the stone-flagged hall. Having reached the bottom stair she stood hesitating for several seconds, uncertain which way to go, but then she caught the sound of voices, and realised that at one end of the hall a door was standing open. The room beyond the door was brightly lit, and deciding that this must be the place where family and guests were expected to assemble before dinner, she made her way towards it.

55

Pausing on the threshold, Susanna hesitated. Suddenly she felt uncertain. The Marquis was standing by one of the room's long windows, his back to the door; his aunt, her body rigidly erect and only her neat dark head slightly bent, was engrossed in a piece of fine embroidery. For nearly half a minute Susanna stood there, unnoticed, but then all at once the Marquis swung round, and across the width of the room his expressionless dark eyes met Susanna's slightly troubled blue ones.

'Ah, Miss Baird!' She could have sworn that he recoiled slightly, but he recovered fairly quickly, and moved forward to place a chair for her.

'I believe you have met my aunt?'

'Yes, we met this afternoon.' She smiled warmly at the Signurina, whose glance was hovering uneasily between the English girl and her nephew. There was a moment's silence, and then Susanna added: 'I met your little boy, too.'

Again there was a short pause, and then the Marquis said slowly: 'So I understand.'

As Susanna sat down he stood watching her. She was wearing a long-skirted dress of silver-grey pleated chiffon, and it gave her very much the look of a dryad, but somehow she didn't think he was studying her appearance. He offered her a drink, and refusing anything stronger she asked for a bitter lemon.

The room was long and beautiful—stone-flagged like the entrance hall, and filled with a magnificent collection of Maltese and Italian antiques. Chair covers, rugs, and the curtains hanging still undrawn beside the six tall, arched windows were all coolly green, like the furnishings in Susanna's bedroom, and there was the same feeling of timeless tranquillity in the air. If it hadn't been for the presence of her host, she would have found it a very soothing room, and would have enjoyed sitting back and absorbing its peace. But her host's presence was something it was difficult to forget, especially when he selected a chair near to her and sat down, without once relaxing the scrutiny to which he had subjected her from the moment of her entering the room.

'My son,' he said suddenly, 'is not used to strangers.'

She flashed him a look, and although she genuinely tried to suppress it a spark of hostility showed in her eyes.

'Yes, I realised that.'

He sensed her disapproval, and as he leant back in his chair a faintly sarcastic smile touched his lips. 'The outside world contaminates, Miss Baird. The more pliable and impressionable one is—the younger one is —the more it contaminates. My son is being most carefully educated. He is being reared in the belief that life is to be lived in accordance with a rigid code of principles. I don't wish him to mix too freely with other human beings until those principles have had an opportunity to become part of him—until his character is fully formed.'

Susanna stared at him, her eyes wide and almost disbelieving. 'But you can't . . . I think that's dreadful!'

He shrugged. 'When you acquire children of your own you will no doubt bring them up in your own way. My son, however, is my responsibility.'

At that moment her grandfather came into the room

and the conversation ended, but Susanna felt shaken. What, in the years ahead, was going to happen to that scrap of humanity who had had the misfortune to be born into this extraordinary household? He couldn't, she decided, be more than eight or nine years old— was he to be kept in seclusion until he became adult? How many other strange ideas were distorting his father's outlook on life?

The dining-room at the Casa de Säez was a long room situated at the back of the house. White-walled, stone-flagged and a little austere, it had something of the look of a monastic refectory, especially as the furnishings were rather sparse. But the gleaming Spanish oak dining-table was loaded with silver and glass, and the dinner itself was lavish. The Marquis and her grandfather soon became absorbed in some of the topics that interested them both, and if conversation between the two women tended to lag sometimes, it never died away altogether, for Susanna was skilful at drawing people out, and for some reason her host's shy, slightly neurotic aunt had aroused her sympathy from the start. She was sure the older woman was worried about Minu—perhaps in time she might even be persuaded to discuss the problem.

Immediately after dinner the Marquis took Robert Debenham into his study for the purpose of inspecting some treasured early record of the de Säez family, and shortly after that, realising how much the Signurina would like to be able to retire to bed, Susanna announced that she herself felt tired. She even pretended to stifle a small yawn, and was amused to see the other woman's face brighten.

58

'You wish to go to bed now?' Marthese inquired with quaint directness.

Susanna allowed her eyelids to droop a little. 'I am tired tonight, as a matter of fact.'

At the foot of the stairs they parted, for Marthese was going to the kitchen for a last-minute talk with Carmen about menus for the following day, and, rather slowly, Susanna went on up to her room.

It was a brilliant moonlit night—although she hadn't realised the fact before—and when she entered her bedroom she found everything bathed in unearthly silver light. No curtains had been drawn across either of the windows, and going across to one of them she looked out at the fairy-tale splendour of the moonlit gardens. They were almost unbearably beautiful ... the leaves of the roses touched with silver, the cypresses tall and black against the indigo sky.

All at once a strange feeling crept over her ... a feeling of loneliness, of being neglected—of being unwanted. Then almost immediately she felt taken aback by her own thoughts. What on earth was the matter with her? Naturally, her grandfather had his own interests—in any case, she ought to be used to his habits by this time. And surely ... surely she didn't expect Ramiro St Vincent de Säez to feel any desire for her company?

She decided she really must be more tired than she had thought, and went to bed. But for a very long time the moonlight kept her awake, and it was nearly one o'clock before, at long last, she drifted into a rather uneasy sleep.

CHAPTER SIX

When Susanna awoke the following morning it was after nine o'clock, and Carmen was coming into her room with a loaded breakfast tray. Bright April sunshine was streaming through the windows, and she could hear birds twittering.

She sat up, feeling guilty, and pushed silky strands of chestnut hair out of her eyes. It wasn't like her to over-sleep.

'Good morning, miss.' Like Emmanuel, Carmen seemed to smile not only with her lips and eyes, but with every inch of her face. 'You sleep well?'

'Very well,' Susanna assured her. She didn't mention the fact that it had been one o'clock in the morning before she had closed her eyes. She looked at her watch. 'Too well,' she said ruefully. 'I'm sorry—you should have wakened me earlier. I meant to go downstairs for breakfast.'

'No, no. No need go downstairs. Why go downstairs?' Smiling more broadly than ever, Carmen plumped up her pillows and set the tray in front of her. It was a large tray, and it needed to be, for it bore all the trappings of a traditional breakfast, plus a small basket of fresh, warm rolls and a pot of steaming coffee. There was quite a selection, too, of different marmalades and preserves, and in addition a pot of the delicious local honey.

Susanna laughed. 'If I do justice to all this,' she complained, 'I shall never get up at all. Does my grandfather get the same?'

The housekeeper looked shocked. 'No, no—Mister Debenham need much bigger breakfast.'

The English girl's eyes widened, then sparkled with amusement. 'Do you really think so?' she asked. 'I'd say he's going to start putting on weight.'

Carmen shook with appreciative laughter and turned to go. Then, with her fingers on the door handle, she paused. 'You like to go for drive?' she asked. 'Is-Signur told Emmanuel to get a car ready for you. It is outside, by the door.' And with another smile she disappeared.

Leaning back against her pillows, Susanna ate her breakfast slowly. The unaccountable depression which had kept her awake for such a long time the night before had evaporated, and she felt curiously at peace with life. After all, she asked herself, what more could she want? Here she was on a beautiful island in the Mediterranean, the weather was warm and brilliant, and on top of everything else a car had been placed at her disposal. A voice inside her remarked that since relations between herself and the car's owner were so strained she definitely ought not to make use of the vehicle, but a few moments' reflection was enough to convince her that circumstances being such as they were, the Marquis would hardly be likely to object if she should get out of his way. Her grandfather, she knew, would not get up until late in the morning, and when he did finally decide to leave his room, he would be unlikely to let her absence disturb him. She supposed she would have to return in time for lunch, but even two or three hours of freedom would be pleasant.

She got out of bed, took a quick shower in the adjoining bathroom, and then slipped into a pretty apple-green cotton which couldn't have been better suited to the glory of the morning. Then she went quietly downstairs and let herself out through the front door.

Sure enough, there was the car. It was a gleaming, cream-coloured Lotus sports model, and it looked almost new. There was no doubt about it, Ramiro St Vincent de Säez was not in the habit of stinting himself when it came to personal comforts. The keys were in the ignition, and it was all ready for use.

But just as she was about to slide into the driving seat, she hesitated. There was a faint scent of roses in the air, and a short distance away, in a lemon tree, a bird was singing its heart out. She remembered that she hadn't yet seen the whole of the garden; and acting on a sudden impulse she closed the door of the car and wandered away to explore. She soon found a small wrought iron gate that led through into what she had already named the 'enchanted garden', and for about twenty minutes she wandered about among the olives and cypresses, inhaling the scent of the flowers and wondering at the age of the place. She looked around for Minu, but then she remembered that he would not be free, and it occurred to her to wonder where his nursery was, and in what part of the house he learnt his lessons. Wherever he was, she supposed the dogs, Simba and Julian, must be with him, for they didn't seem to be anywhere about, and in fact she hadn't seen them since the previous evening, when they had disappeared down the orange grove in pursuit of their small master. She felt glad that at least he had the dogs to keep him company.

She was curious to find out what lay behind the house. She had an idea that there must be some sort of terrace. And there might, she thought, be an interesting view.

But she wasn't in any way prepared for the lonely, romantic beauty of the valley that, falling away below the Casa de Säez, wound gradually down to the sea. It was a narrow, secret valley, carpeted with wild flowers and alive with birdsong, and at the far end, just visible through the criss-crossed branches of an overhanging carob, she glimpsed the vivid blue of the Mediterranean. As she had suspected, there was a terrace that ran almost the entire length of the house, and as she went to lean on the broad balustrade she decided that nothing could possibly be more excitingly beautiful than the view spread out in front of her.

There was, she noticed, a rough narrow path winding through the valley, and gazing downwards she made the discovery that a steep flight of steps connected this track with the terrace on which she stood. Without hesitating any further she made her way to the head of the steps, and climbing carefully down she set out along the path that led through the valley.

The scent of wild thyme rose around her, and everywhere there seemed to be a gentle murmur of bees ... She remembered having read that even in the days of the Romans this had been the island of honey. She couldn't identify many of the flowers that surrounded her, but when she turned her head to the right and lifted her eyes a little, she saw on the skyline a glorious patch of flaming crimson, and that at least she could recognise as *silla*, or giant clover.

As she sped on down the track she felt light-hearted. The dust beneath her thin sandals was soft and warm, and the sun was warm, too, on her legs and her bare arms. It wasn't hot enough to make her wish that she had brought some sort of covering for her head, or to make walking uncomfortable, but it was gloriously warm, and Susanna felt as if every taut nerve and muscle in her body were relaxing under the influence of the sun.

She had been walking for about ten minutes when the valley started to widen ... and suddenly she was on the beach, and her feet were sinking slightly in soft drifts of warm sand. On either side of her the walls of the valley extended into gently sloping, rocky cliffs. She was in a small, secret cove.

Her first thought, as she walked down towards the edge of the sparkling water, was that she should have brought a swimsuit with her. But then she remembered that it was, after all, only April, and somebody had told her the water was still cold. No Maltese, she had gathered, would contemplate bathing until well into May. Just the same, though, it was tempting.

She sat on a glistening rock and shook her hair back, revelling in the cool touch of the faint breeze that was blowing from the sea. Just for a second, dazzled by the glare, she closed her eyes ...

Then, right beside her, someone coughed, and she opened her eyes with a start.

'I'm sorry.' The grey eyes smiling into hers were faintly quizzical. 'I wasn't sure whether you were quite real, you see, and just saying "good morning" doesn't seem the right way of addressing a water-nymph.'

The man standing in front of her was about thirty, and it struck her at once that he looked as if he had not been well. His face was thin and a little haggard for one thing, and if his eyes were kind and humorous they also had a look of being rather haunted. Thick brown wavy hair which had been ruffled considerably by the breeze did lend a rather boyish touch to his appearance, but there was nothing boyish in the lines about his mouth, or in the creases between his eyes.

Susanna stood up, and he made a little gesture of apology.

'Maybe I shouldn't have spoken to you at all ... but as this is a private beach, I just assumed we'd be meeting before long in any case. That's to say, I suppose you're a friend of Ramiro de Säez?'

She pushed a turbulent strand of hair out of her eyes, and surveyed him with curiosity.

'Well, no,' she said frankly. 'As a matter of fact, I'm not. But I am staying in his house.'

The man was gazing at her as if she fascinated him. 'Don't tell me he's kidnapped you?' he persisted, the hint of laughter returning to his eyes. 'I wouldn't have said he was the type. Too morose to think of doing anything so interesting.'

Susanna made an effort to sound prim. 'The Marquis invited my grandfather to stay with him. I just came along because I act as my grandfather's secretary.'

His eyes narrowed thoughtfully, and then he smiled at her. It was a sweet smile, and it transformed his face. 'Does that mean you're Miss Baird?' he asked unexpectedly.

She was surprised, and stared at him for a moment.

'Yes, it does. But how did you know——'

'Put it down to a judicious study of the newspapers, coupled with an ear for gossip. I heard a rumour yesterday that your grandfather might be going to stay at the Casa de Säez.' He broke off. 'I'm sorry—it's time I introduced myself. I'm Peter Hamblyn, and de Säez is my landlord ... for the time being at least.'

'You mean you rent a house from him?' She glanced around at the sparkling sea and the dark, rocky walls of the little cove, almost as if she expected the house in question to materialise on the spot.

'Yes, but it's a mile or so from here. There's a path over the cliffs ... very pleasant on a morning like this. I come here because it's such a peaceful spot, and the right to use this beach goes with my tenancy.'

'Well, I'm sorry I disturbed your morning walk.' She smiled at him, and glanced at her watch. 'I think it's time I was getting back——'

'Oh, now wait a minute! Don't run away.' His lips twisted wryly. 'Before I left England a candid friend was kind enough to inform me that I looked a wreck, but I didn't think I was quite as frightening as all that.' She looked puzzled, and he went on: 'I'm out here to convalesce. Not long ago I was hit by one of those bugs that catch up on you when you least expect it, and apparently I almost went out for the count. The doctors told me I needed a break, and so here I am. I ... I'll be seeing more of you, won't I?'

'I expect so. Do you see very much of the Marquis de Säez?'

'He calls on me sometimes, and I call on him—mainly because he's a mine of information on all things

Maltese. I can't say he's the type I usually get on with, but he's certainly an interesting character. My house, by the way, is the local Taj Mahal ... I daresay you've heard about it.'

Susanna raised her eyebrows. 'Taj Mahal?'

'Well, perhaps that's rather a tasteless sort of joke. Of course the house isn't exactly a tomb or a monument, but it was built for the late Marquesa. It was intended to be the perfect shrine for her matchless beauty, and undoubtedly it must have cost a fortune to build.'

Impelled by curiosity, Susanna asked: 'Was she very beautiful?'

'Well, of course, I didn't know her, but I've been here long enough to hear a good deal about her, and as a matter of fact her portrait hangs in my dining-room. She was a very striking girl. Her death seems to have knocked de Säez endways.'

Susanna remembered the Marquis's face, a face never touched by warmth, softness or humour, and she tried to imagine its owner as he might have been in the days before the tragic loss of an adored wife destroyed something vital inside him. Peter Hamlyn interrupted her.

'I'm going to ask de Säez if he'll bring you over to my place for a drink. Your grandfather, too, of course. Will you come?'

She smiled at him a little absently. 'Yes—yes, of course, I'd like to very much.'

'Marvellous. I'll telephone your host, and fix something up.'

Roughly a quarter of an hour later she arrived back

at the Casa de Säez, and as by that time it was too
late in the morning to think about setting off for a drive
she filled in the short time remaining before lunch by
typing one or two essential business letters for her
grandfather. Punctually at one o'clock a light but pleasant meal was served in the dining-room, but both host
and hostess turned out to be absent, and Susanna realised that in point of fact she need not have felt obliged
to return to the house for a midday meal. Her grandfather was spending the day in his room, browsing over
plans for the research he was about to embark upon,
and as she sat in solitary dignity at the long dining-
table she felt lonely and ridiculous . . . if it had not been
for the fact that Carmen quite obviously enjoyed fuss-
ing over her she would even have felt guilty.

Why, she wondered, was this strange household so
disconcerting?

After lunch she went to see her grandfather, but
finding him absorbed in a book lent him by the Marquis, she soon left him alone, and went downstairs
again to take belated advantage of the chance to drive
the gleaming vehicle still waiting for her outside the
front door. She had no very clear idea where she might
go, but it was a wonderful afternoon, and just following one of the winding white roads that ran down into
the valleys would be an adventure in itself.

But when she finally emerged into the forecourt in
front of the house, she was surprised to find that the
nearside door of the Lotus was standing open, and one
of the large dogs which she had encountered that afternoon was leaning in a nonchalant manner against the
front bumper. She stood still for a moment, and then

caught sight, through the windscreen, of a small dark head. Investigating further, she found that Minu was seated cross-legged in the front passenger seat.

'Well, hello.' She slid into the car beside him. 'Do you want to come for a drive?'

He looked up at her uncertainly, and she noticed that his large, beautiful eyes were remarkably like his father's.

'I was just sitting here. I don't usually go out in the car.' His voice was a reluctant whisper.

Susanna felt anger surge up inside her. This child's life was Dickensian. Something ought to be done— would have to be done—about it. Aloud, she said: 'Well, is anyone going to be angry if you do? Have you finished your lessons?'

'Yes.' He thought for a moment. 'I did English and Latin and geography and maths.'

'With Brother Bernard? You like him, don't you?'

The small head nodded vigorously. 'He's the nicest person I know.'

Impulsively, Susanna almost asked how Minu's father rated in his personal estimation, but she thought better of it immediately. Instead, she smiled at him and then got out of the car again.

'Just wait a few minutes, Minu. I'm going to see if I can take you out with me.'

The Signurina de Säez, like her nephew, was still out, but Carmen was available, and she seemed to see no reason at all why the English guest should not take her employer's small son out for a drive. On the contrary, she obviously felt a motherly sympathy with the neglected child, and thought it an excellent idea that

69

he should have a chance to get out for a while.

Back behind the steering wheel, however, Susanna soon made the discovery that one didn't take Minu out without taking two other passengers as well. The little boy obviously had no intention of going anywhere at all without Simba and Julian, and, equally, Simba and Julian clearly had no intention of being left behind. But there was plenty of room in the back of the car for the two dogs, and once they were settled in their places, their manners seemed to be impeccable. Susanna only hoped that neither of them had any difficult tendencies about which she was not being told.

The car was in perfect order, and beautifully easy to handle. Smoothly, they slipped down the drive until they reached the old stone piers that guarded the entrance ... and then Susanna slowed, and glanced at Minu. The child's face was alight with something like ecstasy.

'Where shall we go?' she asked. Birds were singing in the olive trees, the sky above was the colour of English bluebells, and as they passed through the gateway, she, too, had felt the thrill of freedom.

Minu hesitated, stole a glance at her, and then looked away again. 'I don't mind,' he whispered. Then he added: 'There's a nice place by the sea. It's called Gnejna. Brother Bernard took me there.'

'All right, then.' She smiled encouragingly. 'How do we get there?'

'I'll show you. I remember,' he said proudly.

And it seemed he really did remember, for he directed their progress through a maze of rocky lanes which would have baffled Susanna completely. She didn't know how long it was since he had travelled that way with the monk who supervised his studies, but evidently every detail of the expedition had become engraved upon his memory. At last they came out on to a fairly good road, and almost immediately began to plunge down a hill that came alarmingly close to being perpendicular. On either side of them the sloping fields were ablaze with clover, crimson against the sky. The combination of colour, Susanna thought, was like an assault upon the sense. But there was more to come, for suddenly they rounded a corner, and there was the sea ... the wide, sparkling, azure Mediterranean.

The road continued to run steeply downhill almost until it reached the beach, but then it suddenly levelled out into a large stony area—a space which at the height of the tourist season, Susanna decided, would probably be jammed solidly with parked cars. At the moment, though, there was only one vehicle parked there —a small cream-coloured Volkswagen—and the beach appeared to be deserted.

She looked at Minu. 'Do you want to walk on the beach?' she asked. For the first time she felt slightly uneasy. After all, she didn't think she herself would be able to carry him, even for a short distance, and there didn't seem to be anyone else about. All at once, it occurred to her that in bringing him down to this lonely place she had taken rather a lot upon herself.

But one glance at Minu's face was enough to tell her that he knew exactly what he wanted to do, and that to disappoint him—unless disappointment were unavoidable—would be cruel.

'I want to go over there.' He pointed towards the other side of the bay. 'Brother Bernard took me.'

As it turned out, he walked quite well on the yielding carpet of pale brown sand that stretched down towards the shining water, and Susanna began to relax. The two dogs came with them, never straying very far away, and she felt glad of their company. There were quite a lot of interesting things to take note of, and Minu evidently felt it his duty to act as guide. Brother Bernard, obviously, never missed an opportunity of instruction, and his pupil clearly had quite a gift for absorbing knowledge. He pointed to an ancient stone watch-tower at the top of the cliffs, and explained that it had once been used by soldiers.

'I think it was because of the turkeys,' he told Susanna, gazing up at her seriously.

She stifled a laugh. 'Perhaps you're thinking of the Turks,' she suggested with equal seriousness.

Obviously reluctant to relinquish the turkeys, he looked doubtful, but then another object of interest caught his eye, and he remembered his duty.

'That's Gozo,' he said suddenly, and pointed out across the sea.

Susanna looked in the direction indicated by his small finger, and noticed for the first time that about two miles away across the glittering water there was visible a clearly defined stretch of violet-tinted coastline. It was a coast guarded, she could see, by very tall cliffs, and at one point there was what looked like a large church with a massive dome. So that was Gozo, Malta's tiny sister island.

'Have you ever been there?' she asked Minu.

He shook his head. 'No. But Brother Bernard says he'll take me. When—when my father says I can go.'

It wasn't long before it emerged that for the present moment Minu's particular ambition was to get to a certain rock pool in which he and Brother Bernard had apparently been able to watch quite a lot of interesting fish. Brother Bernard's knowledge of fish, it seemed, was profound, and he knew all their names—even the names of the funny, small things that lurked in the crevices of the rocks. He had told his charge that some people could talk to fish—could call them up to the surface and talk to them just as if they were people—and ever since that day Minu had evidently been burning to put the idea to the test.

Besides, he told Susanna, the pool was nice because it was so clear, and you could see everything—even the sand at the bottom, and the shells.

The snag was that in order to get to the pool one had to cross quite a wide expanse of rock. The rocks were fairly smooth, and there weren't many breaks between them, but just the same ... Susanna looked at Minu's twisted foot, and sighed. It was tragic that he should be prevented from doing a simple thing like this, but on the other hand ...

'Do you think we really ought to go across there?' she asked tentatively. 'I mean, it's bumpy, and——'

'Yes, we must go! Please! It—it isn't bumpy. I can walk ...'

His small, anxious voice trailed away, and glancing down at him Susanna encountered a look of entreaty that caught at her heart. The dogs had come close to them, and they too seemed to be reproaching her.

'All right.' She smiled. 'Give me your hand, and hold on tight.'

As it turned out, it wasn't as difficult as she had expected, and Minu, she discovered, was really quite nimble, having already acquired quite a lot of skill in managing his deformed foot. It wasn't long before they reached the pool, and with Simba beside him he settled down awkwardly to gaze with evident rapture into the glimmering depths. The water really was translucent, and there were quite a lot of fish to be seen—though not as many, Minu reported with slight disappointment, as there had been on the day he had watched them with Brother Bernard. Obviously not wanting Susanna to feel out of things, he supplied her with a lot of information about the various creatures they did see, and when at last something really interesting swam into his line of vision, he clearly expected her to feel just as much excitement as he did himself. Unfortunately, whatever it was that had caught his attention swam out of sight again almost immediately, disappearing into the mysterious blackness beneath an overhanging rock, and he struggled to his feet in order to move sideways to a better point of vantage.

Afterwards she felt convinced that if she had only been prepared for his sudden movement she would have been able to do something to prevent what happened. But as it was, she was utterly unprepared, and it was only when his small body crumpled and his face turned white that she realised something was very wrong. And then she saw that his foot—his twisted right foot—had caught in a crevice, and was being held in what was probably an agonising grip.

'Minu!' Desperately trying to think what was the best thing to do, she put an arm round him, supporting him. 'Minu, can you move your foot?'

He opened his mouth, but no sound came. Helpless tears poured down his cheeks, and he shook his head.

'Well then, darling, I'm going to try and get it out for you. Just keep very still, and be as brave as ever you can.'

But the trapped foot, she soon discovered, was held in a firm grip, and she struggled to subdue a sensation of rising panic. The child, she knew, was in great pain, and her efforts were making matters worse. If he should lose consciousness ... On the other hand, the foot had to be freed. Very gently, but with fingers that trembled violently, she worked on, reproaching herself all the time for her own lack of responsibility in bringing the situation about. If only they hadn't come to the beach ...

And then, suddenly, the small limb was free. Minu was moaning slightly, and his breath came in short, uneven gasps, but he was still conscious, and that was the main thing. On the other hand, the worst clearly wasn't over yet, for when she tried to lift him, he was too heavy for her, and she realised that, as she had feared, she couldn't possibly move him herself. Desperately, she looked around ... and it was then that she became aware of the young couple moving slowly by the water's edge.

She didn't like leaving Minu, even for a minute or two, but in the circumstances it couldn't be avoided, and she didn't have to go very far before she succeeded in attracting the attention of the two people walking on the sand—who up till that moment had clearly been engrossed mainly in one another. They turned out to be German tourists—probably, she decided automatically, a honeymoon couple—and the husband, who spoke excellent English, was only too eager to help. Tall and blond and athletic-looking, he lifted Minu as easily as he might have lifted a baby, and in no time at all the crippled child was being lowered carefully back into the front seat of the Lotus.

The German girl looked sympathetically at Susanna. 'Fraülein, would you like us to come with you ... until you find the doctor?'

Susanna smiled gratefully, but shook her head. 'Thanks, but I'm taking him straight home.' She added ruefully: 'He belongs to somebody else, and I think he had better see his own doctor. If you could tell me your name, though, and where you live ... I'm sure his father will want to write and thank you.'

Pride, she reflected, if nothing else, would ensure that the Marquis wrote to them.

Protesting that they wanted no thanks, and looking rather anxiously through the window at Minu, they waved her goodbye, and she was on her own again. Her one idea was to get back to the Casa de Sáez as quickly as possible, and it was not until they reached the top of the hill leading up from the beach that she suddenly realised that she didn't know the way back. Minu, normally, could have told her, but Minu was huddled, white-faced, in his seat, and he hardly answered when she spoke to him.

She stopped the car and put an arm around him. He

was shivering slightly and his eyes were black with pain. Praying that the ankle wouldn't turn out to be broken—and that he wouldn't develop any serious complications—she started to talk soothingly.

'Listen, darling, we'll soon be home, and you'll feel much better when you're tucked up in bed. But I don't know the road very well, so do you think you could try and tell me which way to go? It isn't very far, is it?'

'N-no.' He let his head drop against her shoulder, and he seemed slightly more relaxed. 'I know the way,' he whispered, 'I'll tell you.'

'There's a good boy.' She let him go on leaning against her, and gradually he seemed to grow a little calmer. The need to concentrate on the road ahead helped to take his mind off his ankle for part of the time, at least, and all in all the drive turned out to be much less nerve-racking than she had expected it to be.

By the time they turned in through the gates of the Casa de Säez, it was after five o'clock, and the sun was beginning to sink, throwing a faint pink light on to the old walls and making a fairyland of the half-seen garden. Susanna knew that at any minute now she was going to have to start offering explanations that could be awkward, but she wasn't worried about that. Anxiety over Minu had driven every other consideration right out of her head, and she could think of nothing now, but what the doctor might be going to say.

And so the sight of her host's grey Jaguar, parked outside the front door, filled her with relief rather than apprehension, and even when she saw that de Säez himself was just climbing out of it she still felt

77

no twinge of nervousness. Instead, gently detaching herself from Minu, she jumped out and ran towards him.

He stood still, watching her approach with a look on his face that was anything but welcoming, and by the time they were face to face with one another some of her courage was beginning to evaporate a little. But Minu was still uppermost in her mind, and she lost no time in coming to the point. As briefly and clearly as possible she told him what had happened, and when he still stood staring at her with hardly any expression on his face, she went on quickly:

'Can you get a doctor here as soon as possible? And somebody must carry him into the house. I—I don't know whether the ankle is sprained or broken, but it's very painful. He's been terribly brave, but——' Something in his eyes made her break off, and she swallowed. 'I ... I'm so sorry,' she finished weakly. 'So terribly sorry.'

'So you said before,' he said icily. 'It doesn't make a great deal of difference. Is Min—is Lorenzo in the car?'

'Yes. If—if somebody could carry him upstairs I'll go with him.' She turned away, intending to hurry back to the Lotus, but she was stopped by the voice of Ramiro de Säez.

'Please, Miss Baird ... if it isn't too much to ask, would you go to your room?'

Susanna stared at him in the fading light. 'But ...' she began helplessly.

'Lorenzo will be taken care of. I realise, of course, that you are a guest in my house, but these circumstances,' he said drily, 'are rather exceptional.'

Anger rose up in her, followed almost immediately by an urge to justify herself—and, finally, by an absurd desire to burst into tears. She glanced back towards the car, feeling desperately sorry for Minu. And then, after hesitating just a moment longer, she turned and walked back into the house.

CHAPTER SEVEN

FOR over an hour Susanna sat alone in her room, staring out at the darkening garden. Her grandfather, she had discovered, was fast asleep in his chair, and in any case she didn't feel like talking to anybody. She didn't really blame the Marquis de Säez for being furious with her—it was the first time she had seen him betray anything in the way of a natural reaction—but at the same time the cold violence of his attitude had upset her more than she would have thought possible. Of course, it didn't matter what he thought of her, but ... strange, how anger could hurt.

She knew by instinct that he wouldn't say anything to her grandfather, and by experience that nothing she could say would induce Robert Debenham to cut his stay short. How she was going to endure the next few weeks she didn't quite know, but—well, anyway, it didn't really matter. The thing that mattered was Minu, and whether or not his ankle was going to be all right. That was the thought that tortured her, as she waited alone in her bedroom ... and whether or not

Ramiro de Säez was being just or even rational in his treatment of her, she knew very well that she was going to find it hard to forgive herself for what had happened that afternoon.

At last there was a knock on the door, and Carmen appeared. She looked as if she had been crying, for her eyes were tinged with red and there were moist streaks on her tanned cheeks. But now she was smiling, and without the least hesitation or self-consciousness she went straight to Susanna and laid a comforting hand on her arm.

'It's all right,' she said reassuringly. 'Everything all right. He's not very much hurt.'

'Isn't he?' Susanna swallowed. 'Are you—are you sure?'

'Yes, sure.' The round brown face was beaming at her. 'Doctor Cutajar has gone. Now he wants to see you. Come along, miss—come and see him.'

Impulsively, Susanna started forward, but then she remembered something. 'I—I don't think——' she began.

Understanding twinkled in the Maltese woman's eyes. 'Is-Signur sent me himself,' she stated firmly.

Feeling bewildered, relieved, and slightly breathless, Susanna allowed herself, without any further argument, to be escorted upstairs to the night nursery, which turned out to be situated on the floor above. On the way up she had an apprehensive feeling that once there she might be forced to come face to face once again with the Marquis himself, but this fear proved groundless, and when Carmen ushered her into the softly lit room there was no one there at all. No one, that is, but the small figure lying quietly in the narrow, white-painted bed.

Minu had obviously been given a sedative and was getting drowsy, but there was no doubt but that he was pleased to see her. The almost beatific smile that crept over his small face was proof enough of that, and when she sat down beside him he gave vent to a contented little sigh.

'I ... wanted ... you to come.' The words came slowly, for he was nearly asleep.

'Did you? Well, here I am. And now you can go to sleep, can't you?' She didn't ask him how he felt, for the pain in his ankle had obviously been relieved, and she decided it would be best not to remind him of it.

'My father was here.' The small voice was getting fainter. 'I ... told him I ... wanted you to come.' An almost inaudible sigh. 'He was nice.'

Susanna felt slightly shaken, but she made a quick recovery, and after only a tiny pause said softly: 'Of course he was nice. He loves you very much.'

She didn't know quite why she said it, but it did seem the best thing to say to the child.

Minu's eyes closed. 'Does ... does ...?' he began. And then his voice was lost in sleep.

On impulse, she bent and very lightly kissed him, then stood up and tiptoed softly to the still open door. And it was only when she reached it that she saw the shadowy figure who had been standing there.

Ramiro de Säez beckoned her out into the brightly lit passageway, and then, soundlessly, he closed the door on the night nursery.

'Miss Baird ...' She looked very much as if she

might be poised for flight, and he put out a hand as if to detain her. There was something strange in his eyes ... something strange and unreadable that she hadn't seen before. 'Miss Baird, I owe you an apology.'

'No, you don't.' She had regained something of her customary composure, and as she looked up at him her eyes were very clear and candid. 'You don't owe me anything. I took your little boy out without your permission, I allowed him to clamber over rocks, and as a result he had a nasty accident. When you realised what had happened you were very angry, and no one could have had more justification. I—I think what I did was unforgivable.'

The sincerity of her contrition showed in her face, and its effect on the man gazing down at her was startling. All at once the dark eyes were as soft as velvet, and when he smiled she saw that a feeling of warmth had reached his eyes.

'That's a very generous speech,' he said. For a moment she had the feeling he was laughing at her. 'But,' he went on, 'you must still accept my apology. My treatment of you this afternoon would have been unforgivable under any circumstances—even if Minu had been seriously hurt.' In answer to the question in her eyes, he added: 'The ankle is sprained, nothing more. He will not even have to rest it for very long. He was frightened, of course—but not nearly as frightened, I think, as he would have been if you had not been with him.' Again that gentle smile. 'He has formed quite an attachment to you. I think—but of course it can only be a guess—that you come close to being more important than the dogs!'

Susanna found it difficult to think of anything to say. She saw that he was holding out his hand to her. 'In England, when you want to make peace with someone ... you shake hands, don't you?'

She gave him her hand like an obedient child, and his slim brown fingers clasped it firmly for several seconds. When he released it she was conscious of a sensation almost akin to regret.

'I—I'm so glad about Minu,' she said awkwardly. 'Glad that the injury isn't serious, I mean.'

'I know you are.' This time the look in his eyes brought a faint glow of colour to her cheeks. And then he glanced briefly at his watch. 'I have to go now—someone is coming to see me at seven. But we'll meet again at dinner.'

He smiled at her, hesitated for a second, and then turned to walk briskly away along the corridor. Susanna was left feeling rather light-headed.

Dinner that evening was a cheerful occasion. Still in the same softened mood, Ramiro de Säez was an attentive host, and several times Robert Debenham glanced at his granddaughter with an almost comical bewilderment in his eyes. He might, under certain circumstances, have been inclined to suspect the influence of the wine, but he had already noticed that despite the excellence of the alcoholic refreshments served under his roof the Marquis himself drank very little. In fact, he seemed to have a depressing partiality for mineral water—one taste which the celebrated author felt unable to share with him.

Susanna, her grandfather noticed, was sparkling, and took a far more active part than she normally did in the unexpectedly general conversation. She and Ramiro de Säez appeared to have agreed on some kind of truce ... which was odd, to say the least, considering what had happened to the boy. He himself saw no reason whatsoever to blame Susanna, but from his own observations so far he would definitely have expected de Säez to do so.

The Signurina, it seemed to him, was the only person present whose spirits appeared to have been seriously affected by Minu's accident, and with a sudden urge to be kind he began to concentrate his attention on her.

After dinner, quite unexpectedly, the Marquis suggested that they should all go out on to the terrace, an idea which did not at first seem likely to attract much support. Robert Debenham, who knew very well that the nights were unlikely to be really warm for at least another month, repressed a shudder and said urbanely that after such a fine dinner he didn't honestly think he would be capable of moving so far. Of course, he didn't want to discourage anyone else. Beside him, the Signurina shrugged her insubstantial lace shawl a little more closely about her thin shoulders, and as she did so glanced appealingly at her nephew, as if begging to be excused.

Ramiro looked at Susanna. 'Would you like to come outside?' he asked. His voice was almost shy. 'The moon is almost full ... the view will be spectacular.'

'Yes, I—I'd like to see the view from the terrace.'

She allowed him to usher her out through one of the long windows, and within a second or so they were standing where she had stood earlier in the day, before she set off on her walk through the valley. As the

Marquis had predicted the moon was large and brilliant, very nearly at the full, and the narrow valley below them was bathed in silver light. Through a network of overhanging branches they could glimpse the shimmering sea.

'Oh!' Susanna caught her breath. 'It's—it's wonderful.' Then the cool night breeze touched her, and she shivered.

'Are you cold?' He sounded concerned.

'No, of course not.' She was wearing a light wrap, and she folded it more tightly around her. Strange, she thought, that she should be standing here looking at the moon ... with Ramiro St Vincent de Säez. There had been such hostility between them. Could it really have evaporated so suddenly?

'I hope,' he said quietly, 'you're enjoying your visit to Malta?'

She looked up at him. 'Yes,' she said after a moment, 'anyone would. It's such a beautiful island.' She added quickly: 'It was very good of you to let me use your car this afternoon.'

He made a small dismissing gesture. 'I hope you will use it many times. It will be at your disposal as long as you remain here. Perhaps ...' He seemed to hesitate. 'Perhaps you would sometimes allow me to drive you myself. There's so much that I could show you ...'

He sounded almost eager, and she glanced up at him with quick appreciation. 'But you're so busy—I don't want to take up too much of your time.'

His eyes, dark and unfathomable, gazed straight

85

down into hers, and she became conscious of a strange feeling of breathlessness.

'I can make time,' he said, 'when I want to.'

They leant against the balustrade, and he asked her about her home in England. With a little smile, she confessed that she didn't really have one.

'Grandpapa has a flat in London,' she told him, 'but we don't spend very much time there. We're travelling most of the time.'

'And you don't mind?' He was gazing straight ahead now, towards the sea.

She shook her head slowly. 'Not really. Grandpapa doesn't work so well if he stays in one place for too long, and in any case he gets bored. He did once try staying in London for as much as six months—I think he thought it would be better for me—but he very nearly became impossible to live with.' A soft laughter escaped her. 'I think he's at his happiest when he's just setting out for the airport.'

'He is a remarkable man.' She felt him turn sideways, and knew that he was studying her closely in the moonlight. 'And he's fortunate,' he added slowly. 'Fortunate, I mean, that you have decided to devote yourself to him.'

Suddenly pure pleasure, of a bewildering intensity, bubbled up inside her. But at the same time she couldn't help recalling another occasion ... an occasion upon which her companion had delivered himself of rather different sentiments.

'But you don't think,' she suggested, mischievously, 'that it would be better for him if he didn't see too much of me during the next few weeks?'

Glancing up under her lashes she saw him frown swiftly, and then a sudden smile flashed across his face.

'I said that, did I?'

'Well, you said something of the sort. With the best of intentions, of course! You felt Grandpapa was in need of protection.'

'I apologise.' There was a glint of humour in his eyes.

'Thank you,' she said gravely.

Abruptly, he turned towards her. 'Tomorrow we will both leave him in peace, and I will show you something of Malta. What would you like to see?'

'I ...' She shrugged and smiled, wondering why all at once she should feel so absurdly shy. 'Anything and everything—I haven't seen very much,' she confessed.

'Then we will go and see everything,' he said.

All at once Carmen appeared behind them. Somewhere, in the recesses of the house, a telephone had been ringing, and now she had evidently come to tell Is-Signur that someone wanted to speak to him urgently. Apologising briefly, he disappeared, but Susanna remained on the terrace. It was a wonderful night, and she felt disinclined to go inside and leave it.

Four or five minutes later, Ramiro came back again. He was walking rather slowly, she noticed, and although he didn't look at her immediately she sensed a change in him. Nearly a minute went by before he spoke, and when at last he did his voice was cool.

'That was a neighbour of mine.' He paused, then turned to look at her. 'A tenant, actually.' He seemed to be waiting for something, but she did nothing but gaze at him inquiringly. At last, he said: 'You met him this morning, I think.'

'I met ...?' Bewildered, she forced her mind back. And it was then that, for the first time, she remembered Peter Hamblyn. Somehow so much seemed to have happened during the second half of the day that her meeting with the Englishman had been driven completely out of her mind. 'Oh!' she said rather flatly. 'Yes—I remember.'

'You didn't mention this ... encounter.'

'I'd forgotten about it,' she told him honestly. 'But I remember that Mr—Mr Hamblyn seemed to know you—quite well.' She swallowed and looked up at him. In the clear moonlight his face was like a mask. For some reason that she still couldn't quite fathom his attitude towards herself had undergone another dramatic change, and she felt as if she had swallowed ice, and were chilled to the heart.

'Well, Mr Hamblyn had not forgotten you. Of course, it would be surprising if he had.' The expressionless eyes bored into her. 'He says he told you he would be ringing ... I am to take you to see him. With your grandfather, of course.' A mocking note had invaded his voice.

'Yes—yes, that's right.' She felt ridiculously guilty, without even beginning to know why. 'Does he ... live far away?' she asked mechanically.

He shrugged. 'About five miles away. You had better take the Lotus. It will be just right for your grandfather and yourself. Or perhaps,' on a more conversational note, 'you will decide to go alone?'

'But won't you——' She felt acutely uncomfortable.

'I mean, you'll be going too, won't you?'

'No.' He glanced absently at his watch. 'I have rather a lot on hand at the moment, but I have accepted an invitation on your behalf. You will be expected at six o'clock tomorrow evening.' Without even looking at her again he turned away, towards the lighted windows of the dining-room. 'Perhaps we shall meet tomorrow evening—provided, of course, that you don't decide to have dinner with Mr Hamblyn.'

And then, with a brisk 'goodnight', he was gone, and she was left alone on the terrace.

Susanna didn't sleep well that night. The bed that had been so blissfully comfortable the night before suddenly seemed to be stuffed with rocks, and the white light of the moon tormented her. Once she heard Minu call out and got up to go to him, but she soon realised that both Carmen and Marthese de Säez were on their way to the night nursery on the top floor, and as their hurrying footsteps died away up the stairs she got back into bed. She was, after all, a complete outsider and it wasn't for her to interfere.

As she lay, tossing restlessly, in the big shadowy room, her tired mind was a jumble of ill-assorted pictures. But he most persistent among them was the one that showed her Ramiro's face, and the look she had seen in his eyes when he came back from the telephone. The whole of the previous day had been so bewildering ... At the start of it she and the Marquis de Säez had been on terms, almost, of open hostility. But then, with Minu's accident, everything had somehow changed, and ... She had a vision, suddenly, of the warmth in a pair of velvety dark eyes, and in its wake an unaccountable feeling of desolation swept over her.

She supposed it would be childish not to realise that her host's second change of attitude towards her had been due largely to masculine pique—jealousy would be too strong a word. He had been prepared to unbend a little ... probably because it had occurred to him that his dislike of women in general was leading him into unreasonable and slightly ridiculous extremes of hostility, he had decided to get a grip on himself and behave with a little more rationality. As a mark of special condescension he had actually offered to take her on a tour of the Island. But then Peter Hamblyn had telephoned, and he had made the discovery—or thought he had—that she had already, without his knowledge, accepted some sort of invitation from another man ... an invitation which he probably thought she had been deliberately concealing from him.

The worst thing was that she had been beginning to think they might become friends. Well, at least she understood him now, and she wouldn't make the same mistake again. Perhaps ... perhaps her grandfather would complete his Maltese researches fairly quickly, and they wouldn't be staying much longer.

Hating the moonlight, she turned on her side and made an effort to get to sleep.

She awoke in the morning with a headache, and felt half guilty, half relieved, when she found that Carmen was once again knocking on her bedroom door with a loaded breakfast tray. She hadn't much appetite for the breakfast, but she was grateful for the fact that she didn't have to go straight down to the dining-room.

Later she heard that the Marquis had gone out, and was not expected back until very late that evening. It didn't surprise her in the least that his plans for taking her on a tour of the Island should have been abandoned so promptly ... The only thing that did surprise her was that she herself felt so oddly flat. Putting her feelings down to the after-effects of an exceptionally bad night, she made her way up to the nursery.

Minu was wide awake and his injured ankle didn't seem to be giving him too much trouble, but by the time Susanna made her appearance he was feeling bored, and becoming mildly fretful. Marthese de Säez probably had no time to spare for sitting with him, and Carmen certainly hadn't, so he was quite by himself. Sitting down on the bed, Susanna picked up one of the books with which he was surrounded and glanced at it. It was *The Wind in the Willows*.

'Have you read this book, Minu?' she asked.

He nodded gravely. 'Yes.' At the sight of her his face had brightened.

'Do you like it?'

'Yes.' He hesitated, then added: 'But we don't have many animals here ... only rats and hedgehogs.'

She smiled. 'I didn't know there were any hedgehogs in Malta.'

'Oh, yes,' he assured her quickly, 'there are. We have two in our garden. They're called Hannibal and Giuza.'

'What nice names,' she said seriously. 'I'd love to meet them.'

Minu's brow puckered. 'But they only come out at night,' he objected. 'I see them, because sometimes

91

when Carmen knows they're in the garden she lets me go down to look. But only if it's just getting dark ... not if it's late.'

'Well,' said Susanna, 'we must ask them to supper.'

Minu's small, neat features dissolved into an ecstatic smile, and he wriggled delightedly. 'I like you,' he announced suddenly, 'I like you almost better than anybody.'

Susanna spent the rest of the morning with him, and later on, when he had had his afternoon nap, she went back to the nursery and stayed with him until a little after five o'clock, when she suddenly remembered— for the first time that day—that she and her grandfather were supposed to be going out. She would have given a lot to be able to get out of the arrangement, but that wasn't possible. Excuses were out of the question —there was nothing she could say that wouldn't strike Ramiro de Säez as being an obvious lie, and he might even get the idea that she had decided to snub Peter Hamblyn in order to please him. That would be unbearable. Besides, rather to her surprise, her grandfather wanted to go.

Peter Hamblyn's house—or rather, the house he rented from the Marquis de Säez—was situated near Dingli, on the only part of the Island's coastline where cliffs rise to terrifying heights, and where the view is breathtakingly spectacular. On a brilliant summer morning, Susanna guessed, it would be a wonderful and exciting place to be. But by the time she and her grandfather arrived, dusk was beginning to fall, and a light evening haze lay over the sea, giving a feeling of loneliness and mystery which was a little chilling. Wide iron gates guarded the short, curved drive which led up through massed oleander bushes to the front door of the house, and as the car slipped through she glimpsed a name : Villa Célèstine.

The house was white and sprawling, strikingly beautiful in the architectural tradition of ancient Greece. A terrace, paved with vivid mosaics, stretched the entire length of the building, and everywhere there seemed to be rounded arches and graceful Doric columns. Not only must it have cost a great deal to build, but quite obviously great care and imagination had gone into the planning of every detail. Célèstine ... Had that been the name of Ramiro's wife?

Peter Hamblyn was waiting to welcome them, and it was clear that he had been looking forward enthusiastically to their visit—though the fact that Ramiro de Säez had been unable to come didn't seem to upset him too much. He was delighted to make the acquaintance of Robert Debenham, and for his part the celebrated author was gratified to discover that Peter was a dedicated admirer of his books. For more than half an hour, seated comfortably in a long white-and-gold reception room overlooking the darkening sea, they talked about books, and seeing that her grandfather was in his element Susanna was perfectly happy to relax in one corner of a deep settee and say almost nothing.

She couldn't help noticing, though, that her host's eyes constantly wandered in her direction, and while the literary lion was temporarily occupied with a local newspaper cutting which Peter had thought might interest him, he seized the opportunity to speak to her for a moment.

'Are you settling in happily at the Casa de Säez?' As he spoke there was a flicker of whimsical humour in his eyes.

'The Marquis looks after his guests very well.' Her voice was quiet, her expression rather difficult to read.

'I ...' He hesitated a moment, and then he grinned openly. 'I rather got the impression—from the way you talked about him the other day—that you and he don't hit it off all that well.'

She shrugged. It was a convincingly casual shrug. 'I don't really know him. Grandpapa sees a lot more of him than I do.'

'Sounds as if you're being neglected, and that won't do, you know. I was wondering ...' He hesitated again, smiling at her. 'Would you think of having dinner with me one evening? There are plenty of attractive night-spots around—it doesn't have to be the Grand Hotel Melita!'

He was watching her eagerly—looking, she thought, a little like a friendly, anxious spaniel. But thinking quickly she made the discovery that, nice as he was, she didn't want to have dinner with Peter Hamblyn. She glanced at her grandfather. They had a private arrangement which was specially designed to cover situations of this sort.

'Well, I—I'd love to,' she felt guilty already, 'but I shall have rather a lot of work on hand during the next few weeks ... shan't I, Grandpapa?'

Robert Debenham, who had fortunately surfaced in

time to get the gist of the conversation, nodded emphatically.

'I do my best work in the evenings,' he remarked cheerfully, 'and Sue will be taking dictation every evening for a month. I'm getting started tomorrow. If, after that, I miss a single evening's work, I shall lose the thread completely. Of course, after one month I shall take a rest.' He smiled expansively. 'Sue will be quite free then.'

The younger man raised his eyes in astonishment. 'But, Mr Debenham, surely you could spare her for one evening!'

'Not for half an evening,' his guest assured him tranquilly. 'She's quite indispensable.' In a tone of polite inquiry, he added: 'You'll be here in a month's time?'

'I believe so.'

'Well then,' placidly, 'that's all right!'

Before leaving they were taken into the dining-room of the Villa to admire the magnificent, glowing portrait of the tragic young Marquesa St Vincent de Säez. It showed a beautiful, slender girl in her early twenties, with a delicate, piquant face and enormous, frightened dark eyes. She had been painted in a brightly coloured, insubstantial summer dress, and her thick black hair fell about her shoulders like a cloak.

'Good-looking girl,' Robert Debenham remarked. He was studying the portrait with dispassionate interest.

Peter Hamblyn looked at Susanna. 'What do you think?'

'I think she must have been very beautiful.' The answer came quickly, but something about the painting had made her feel cold inside, and she turned away.

On the doorstep Peter repeated his dinner invitation. 'Please try to get away,' he said coaxingly, his warm grey eyes on her face. 'Your grandfather surely wasn't serious!'

'Well, no,' she admitted. 'He isn't really a taskmaster. But he has got quite a lot of work ahead of him, and it's only fair that I should give him as much support as I can, at least for a week or two. If he wants to work in the evening—and he usually does—I should be on hand to help him.'

'Well, come for a drive one morning, then. Better still, have lunch with me!'

Feeling conscience-stricken, she relented a little. 'I'll try!'

As she got back into the car and turned to say goodbye—her grandfather was already installed in the passenger seat—she was rewarded by a warm smile.

They moved away down the short drive and Robert Debenham shook his head reproachfully. 'I don't see why I should be turned into an ogre, just so that your unwanted admirers can be scared away. That young man has conceived a loathing of me which it might take a lifetime to dispel!'

Susanna smiled. 'Well, I did feel a little bit guilty,' she confessed. 'But you are an ogre, Grandpapa—you know you are!'

He gave vent to a noncommittal grunt. Then, unexpectedly, he asked: 'What's wrong with the boy, anyway? Why won't you have dinner with him? Speaking as a watchful grandparent, I must say that I'd consider him an entirely suitable escort.'

She made a little dismissing movement. 'I ... just don't feel like having dinner with anybody.'

Later, after they had dined alone with Marthese—Ramiro de Säez was not expected back until very late—she pleaded the excuse of a very bad headache, and escaped to her own room shortly after nine o'clock. Once again the world beyond the windows was brilliant with moonlight, and once again she couldn't sleep.

Half unconsciously, she was waiting for the sound of a car—for the gentle hiss of the Jaguar's tyres ... for the thud of a closing door. But no sound at all disturbed the tranquillity of the house, and a little before one o'clock she fell asleep.

CHAPTER EIGHT

DURING the next few days Susanna found herself kept busy most of the time. Her grandfather started work on his book, and wanting to help him as much as possible she spent hours on end typing out numberless draft versions of the first chapters. In actual fact he wasn't at all a taskmaster—and since he dictated mainly on to tapes she was quite free to do most of the necessary typing at any time that suited her. But she wanted to feel occupied—she wanted to be involved in something familiar and satisfying. Although she didn't quite understand why, she didn't want to be left with too much time in which to think.

After the first week of May the weather suddenly changed, and what had seemed to be the steady approach of summer was unexpectedly checked by long days of wind and torrential rain. In the 'secret' garden lakes formed between the hibiscus bushes, and under the orange trees creamy, fallen blossom lay in drifts. The temperature dropped surprisingly, and sometimes, in the evenings, central heating was necessary. Peter Hamblyn telephoned several times, but while the bad weather lasted Susanna had plenty of excuses for not going out with him, and for most of the time she found herself left more or less in peace. Every day she spent an hour or so with Minu, and the two of them struck up a firm friendship, but apart from that she saw hardly anyone but her grandfather. The Marquis apparently had several important business transactions on hand, and his younger guest, at least, saw very little of him.

Until one wet, blustery afternoon towards the middle of May, when, going up unexpectedly to the nursery, he found Susanna engaged in helping his son with a large jigsaw puzzle depicting the battle of Waterloo.

Neither of them noticed him at first, and for several seconds he stood silently in the doorway, watching the two heads bent so close together—one a bright, glowing chestnut, the other as black as the wing of a raven. Then something made Susanna lift her head, and she immediately stood up, looking a little self-conscious.

'I am disturbing you.' He walked slowly into the middle of the room, and stood looking down at the puzzle. 'What is this ... a battle? Do you think Miss Baird likes battles, Lorenzo?'

'Actually,' said Susanna, 'it's very interesting.' He turned to look at her, and she flushed, feeling like a child herself.

'So you do like battles.' There was the suspicion of a smile on his lips. 'Your hair is the right colour. Isn't there a tradition in England about ... hair of that colour?' He stood looking at it for a moment, as if its mildly controversial hue interested him, and then, as she said nothing, he bent over the jigsaw puzzle.

'This is meant to be the battle of Waterloo?' he inquired.

'Yes, Father.' Minu gazed up at him with anxious politeness.

'You have the whole of the Duke of Wellington, I see. But Napoleon has not yet got his hat on.'

'No.' Minu frowned. 'We haven't been able to find his hat. He hesitated. 'He—he doesn't look very bad, does he?'

'Well, should he?' There was a curious expression on the Marquis's face as he stood looking down at his son.

'Brother Bernard says he was a very bad man.' The small face assumed a thoughtful expression. 'Do you think he was, Father?'

Ramiro de Säez seemed taken aback, and he glanced rather ruefully at Susanna. 'Napoleon was a soldier,' he explained carefully, 'and as a soldier he sometimes did bad things.'

With unusual temerity, Minu persisted. 'But was he really bad?' he wanted to know.

This time Susanna answered. 'No one is ever *all* bad, Minu, just as no one is ever completely good. There are little bits of good and little bits of bad in everybody. Only God knows how much good there is in a person —and He's the only one who knows how much bad there is, too. We don't know, and that's why we should never say nasty things about people ... even when they seem to be really wicked. We don't know what has made them do the things they do—only God does.'

Minu gazed up at her with rapt interest. He must, she thought, have heard something of the sort before— at least from Brother Bernard—but just the same the idea seemed to strike him with all the force of novelty. He looked as if he were about to ask something more, but at that moment his father recollected why it was that he had come to the nursery in the first place.

'I was looking for you, Miss Baird.' He glanced across at Susanna. 'Mr Hamblyn telephoned a few minutes ago, but nobody could find you, so he left a message.' The dark eyes became expressionless. 'He is hoping you will go out with him tomorrow—for a drive round the Island.'

'Oh!' said Susanna.

'I imagine you will go? It should be a most interesting experience.'

She hesitated. 'Well, I—I don't know. I don't think so. My grandfather will probably be needing me, and —and in any case ...'

'Yes?' He was watching her closely. 'In any case?'

'I ... well, I rather like exploring by myself,' she said.

His brows lifted. 'You don't think you would enjoy ... exploring with Mr Hamblyn?'

Almost against her will, she felt forced to meet his eyes, which were hard and questioning. There was a short pause. She had been going to say something light and noncommittal, but the words wouldn't pass her lips.

At last she said quietly: 'Not particularly.'

For several seconds there was silence in the room, and for some unaccountable reason she felt as if the air were charged with electricity. Then, unexpectedly, Minu spoke up.

'Father, do you—do you think I could go exploring with Susanna?'

The Marquis looked down at him with a faint flicker of amusement.

'Since you have the privilege of calling her Susanna —which I have not!—perhaps you had better ask her yourself!'

All at once Susanna felt relaxed. She laughed, and knelt down again beside Minu and the jigsaw. 'Of course you can come with me—I don't really want to go alone!'

'Ah!' Ramiro sounded amused. 'Now we are getting to the truth.' Then the amusement faded, and his voice changed. 'I suppose,' he said rather wryly, 'it would spoil everything if I came along too?'

Once again she allowed herself to meet his eyes. They were unfathomable.

'I don't think it would spoil anything,' she told him rather breathlessly. As she spoke she smiled at him.

'Then that is settled.' He cleared his throat and glanced at Minu. 'Do you mind ... Minu?'

The boy flushed. For one thing, he was not used to hearing the name 'Minu' on his father's lips ... and for another, it was probably the first time in his life that the Marquis had consulted him over anything. In the

101

wake of the flush a glow of pleasure spread over his small face.

'I would like it very much, Father.'

'Then tomorrow we will go, if the sun shines. That is all right with you, Miss Baird?'

'Yes, of course.' She added, greatly daring: 'That so-called privilege of Minu's you mentioned ... you can have the same.'

He looked at her quickly, then smiled. 'We will go tomorrow ... Susanna.'

A short time later they left the nursery together, and as the door closed behind them she turned impulsively to face Ramiro.

'I'm so glad you decided to take Minu out. I don't know if you realise how much it will mean to him.'

He looked down at her. 'I am not going simply for the benefit of Minu.'

Susanna coloured. In a tone that was meant to be reproving but didn't quite manage it, she said: 'Well, I think you ought to be.'

Ramiro stood still, frowning. 'You don't sound serious,' he remarked, 'but there is a serious thought behind what you say. Am I such a bad father, do you think?'

'Not a bad father,' she answered gently. 'But perhaps—sometimes—an abstracted one.'

His brows were still drawn together. 'I told you once,' he reminded her, 'that I believed in keeping my son segregated from the world—until such time as his character could be considered to have developed. You were not pleased.'

'No,' she said, 'I wasn't. But I see now that you

really believed it was the best thing for him.'

'You speak in the past tense. Do you think I am about to be converted?'

She looked up at him, and her eyes were serious. 'I'll tell you what I think. I think you love Minu, and you always have, but until recently you didn't really stop to think about him. You felt responsible for him, you wanted the best for him, but when you looked at him you didn't see a real child. You saw your son—a kind of abstract—but not a living human being, with needs and feelings and——' She stopped, seeing a look of withdrawal in his eyes. 'I'm sorry,' she said huskily. Somehow the knowledge that she had hurt him made something inside herself ache dully.

'Please go on.' His voice was rather tense, but he didn't sound angry.

'Well, I was only going to say ...' She hesitated, searching for words. 'I was only going to say that now, at last, I think you're really beginning to see Minu. You're beginning to understand him. And so, in time, you'll understand what is really best for him.'

'And you feel you can trust me to do what is "best" for him—when, at last, I know what that is?' Now his eyes were faintly quizzical, but the tension had gone from him.

Susanna smiled. 'I think so.'

'Well, that's good.' With a brisk change of mood, he glanced at his watch. 'I have to go now, and I shall be out this evening. But tomorrow, if the weather is kind to us, we will make an early start. Minu's ankle grows stronger every day, but I think it will be as well if I carry him down to the car, so perhaps we should meet here—at about nine o'clock?'

Feeling mildly amused by his dictatorial methods, she agreed, and as they parted Ramiro expressed the hope that the following day's weather would come up to expectations.

But as it turned out the next day was wet and very windy, and it was not until the day after that Susanna opened her eyes to a warm, clear morning laden with promise of a golden day to come. Getting out of bed, she ran to the window, and as she leant out the combined scents of roses and orange blossom rose in a cloud from the shimmering garden, just touched by the sun. There was no doubt about it, this was the day for a tour of the Island. Her heart started to beat faster, and she felt as excited as a child on the morning of her birthday.

Just before nine o'clock she went up to the nursery, and shortly afterwards the Marquis arrived. Minu, who was wearing an immaculate white shirt and beautifully tailored long trousers—currently the pride of his existence—was in a state approaching ecstasy, and Carmen, who had been engaged in getting him ready, looked as delighted as if the whole thing had been planned for her own benefit. The Marquis carried his son downstairs, and as the little party emerged into the sunlit forecourt Minu gave vent to a squeak of delight which he obviously found it impossible to repress. For just outside the door the grey Jaguar was drawn up—and for Minu the Jaguar was undoubtedly the next best thing to a ship of dreams.

Very gently he was deposited on the comfortable

rear seat, and the door was closed upon him. Then his father turned to look at Susanna.

She was wearing a shade of blue which did quite unexpected things for her hair, and her eyes were sparkling. At first she met his gaze frankly, but after a moment or two something in it made her look away, and she spoke hurriedly.

'It's a wonderful morning, isn't it? Where are we going?'

There was a pause, and then he said slowly: 'First we will go along the coast to Ghajn Tuffieha and Golden Bay. Then we will go through St Paul's Bay to Marfa, and you will be able to look across to Gozo. After that ... after that, we will return along the coast road to Sliema and Valletta, where there are many things you should see. Then we shall have lunch. And while we are eating our lunch we shall discuss what we ought to do with the afternoon.' He opened the car door for her. 'I want you,' he said softly, 'to know Malta well.'

An hour later, speeding along the magnificent coast road that runs from Salina to St Andrew's, Susanna felt that she was beginning to know Malta very well indeed. From Golden Bay—where the width of the yellow sands reminded her of Cornwall—they had driven to St Paul's Bay, and there she found herself gasping with delight. For spread in front of them like a theatre backcloth a pretty little white town lay huddled around the sparkling waters of a neat, semi-circular bay. And just beyond the last of the houses, separated from the mainland only by a narrow channel, they could see the pearl-grey island on which St Paul had

105

been shipwrecked. From the back seat Minu explained kindly: 'There weren't any houses here then.'

Having left St Paul's Bay they had headed towards Marfa, and there, parking the car beside a mimosa-lined road, they found themselves looking straight across to the island of Gozo—beautiful, mushroom-coloured dreamland floating on an azure sea. They saw the morning ferry-boat leave, cleaving a white path through the waters on her way to Gozo's only port, and Ramiro said suddenly:

'One day we must all go to Gozo. But not today.'

Susanna looked at him and then quickly looked away again. Somehow, for some absurd reason that 'we' had caused her heart to skip a beat.

The Marquis didn't talk much—except to point out landmarks and impart interesting information—but she knew that she had never seen him so relaxed. And she could almost feel Minu relaxing too.

The coast road, which wound like a broad white ribbon along the very edge of the Mediterranean, was a delight from beginning to end. There was no spectacular inland scenery, for this was the flat part of the Island, and the cultivated hillsides of the western coast had given place to an expanse of rocky grey moorland that Susanna thought might easily resemble the surface of the moon. But even the moorland looked beautiful in the sunlight, and the glorious width and blueness of the shimmering sea made her feel as if she had been re-born. Here and there they came upon a smart yacht, riding at anchor in a shallow inlet, and once a lovely white liner, headed for Grand Harbour, drew a gasp of admiration from Minu.

'*Quinquereme of Nineveh*,' Susanne murmured half absent-mindedly, and to her surprise Ramiro completed the quotation.

'*Quinquereme of Nineveh from distant Ophir, rowing home to haven in sunny Palestine ... With a cargo of ivory, and apes and peacocks, sandalwood, cedarwood, and sweet white wine.*' He turned to smile at her. 'To the average person, of course, that ship is only a little Italian liner with a cargo of tourists. But we know better, you and I.'

Astonished to find that he could so easily pick up and sympathise with the romantic, imaginative train of her own thoughts, Susanna turned to him with a spontaneous glow in her eyes. But what she saw in his face made her look away again quickly, and with a heart that had suddenly begun to pound she concentrated all her attention on the liner.

Since the main attraction of Sliema was its shops— particularly its dress-shops—they drove more or less straight through, the Marquis remarking with a smile that he had not the courage to face up to a feminine shopping expedition.

'Besides,' he added, the smile still playing about his mouth, 'there are only twenty-four hours in the day, and when a woman finds herself in a shop that is not always enough. At least, there is not usually time for anything else, and we have other things to do.'

Susanna wondered, fleetingly, whether the beautiful young Marquesa de Säez had been much addicted to visiting elegant dress-shops. Probably, she decided, it had been the couturiers of Paris who had claimed most of Célèstine's attention.

They didn't, after all, go down into Valletta itself, for Susanna had already seen a good deal of the city and Minu was not able to walk far. But for nearly an hour they cruised around the edges of Grand Harbour, and for Minu at least, silently enthralled in the back of the car, this was obviously the highlight of the morning. The dockland areas turned out to be fascinating, for some of the oldest and most interesting buildings on the Island were to be found close to the waterfront, and Susanna learnt that during the great Turkish siege the whole district had fought magnificently. The waterside town of Vittoriosa had been named to commemorate the ultimate Maltese victory ... and neighbouring Cospicua had been so-called in honour of the conspicuous part it had played in the Island's defence. More recently, during the Second World War, the area—like most of the rest of Malta—had once again suffered badly, but the honey-coloured stones were still beautiful, and the narrow, ancient streets held an atmosphere which, Susanna decided, was probably unique in the world.

It was nearly twelve o'clock by the time they came to the end of their tour, and for the first time the Marquis turned slightly, in order to look over his shoulder at his son.

'Hungry?' he inquired briefly.

For a moment Minu seemed rather taken aback. Then he nodded with vigorous enthusiasm. 'Yes, Father!'

'That is good, for we are now going to the Melita, where we shall have lunch. Will you like that?'

Minu leant forward a little. 'You mean—are we

really going to have lunch at the Grand Hotel Melita?' His small voice was husky with awe, and judging by the reverence with which he enunciated every syllable it sounded as if he considered his father's hotel to be well on the road to heaven.

'Yes, we really are.' The Marquis's voice sharpened a little. 'Minu, have you never been there?'

'No, Father.'

Ramiro glanced sideways at Susanna. *Mea culpa,* he murmured. 'Do you think I'm a tyrannical madman?'

She shook her head. 'I've told you what I think.'

'And that includes the conviction that I am about to reform my ideas?'

She turned her clear gaze upon him. 'You are, aren't you?'

There was silence for nearly a minute. Then, briefly, he looked at her. His expression was grave but otherwise unreadable. 'It is not a question of ... reforming,' he said slowly. He seemed to speak with difficulty. 'It is more a question of—coming out of the mist into the sunlight.'

And then they were at the gates of the Grand Hotel Melita, and he changed the subject abruptly, making some comment on the large number of vehicles in his car park. Beside him, Susanna felt confused and shaken, and she said nothing more on any subject until they were all installed in one of the hotel's magnificent cocktail lounges.

In the quietly impressive Grand Masters' Room, which overlooked an inner courtyard, they relaxed for half an hour in an atmosphere of air-conditioned tranquillity. At her host's suggestion Susanna sampled a glass of Kinnie—a bitter-sweet, non-alcoholic local drink with a strong taste of herbs—and although after a few sips she came to the conclusion that the sparkling, reddish-brown liquid was probably rather an acquired taste, she had to admit that it was oddly refreshing. Minu drank Kinnie, too, and as he reclined between Susanna and his father in a massive, comfortable arm-chair it was quite obvious that he felt himself to be in some kind of seventh heaven.

As for the Marquis, he was suddenly relaxed, and Susanna felt herself relaxing in sympathy. For part of the time they talked about England, and Ramiro recalled the very happy years he had spent at a boys' public school in Hampshire. She guessed that it was quite a long time since he had last thought about his own childhood, and when he glanced rather uncertainly at Minu she realised he was wondering, perhaps for the first time, whether it might not after all be a good idea to send his own son to school in England.

'When I was at school,' he said suddenly, 'life seemed to make sense. There was a rhythm, a purpose to it all ... a feeling of well-being, too, that did not often leave one.' He smiled very faintly. 'I really believed that "all was for the best, in the best of all possible worlds".'

'You should go back some time,' she suggested. 'To England, I mean.'

'I do. That is, once or twice a year I go to London on business. But of course, as you are about to tell me'—smiling faintly—'that is not the same thing.'

'It certainly isn't. You can't go back to school, of

110

course, but you could go and pay the Hampshire countryside a visit.'

The Marquis laughed. 'Yes, I suppose I could.' He added curiously: 'You are fond of Hampshire?'

She nodded. 'I love it. An aunt of mine used to live there, and I stayed with her a lot when I was small.'

In the short silence that followed, a small voice suddenly made itself heard.

'I have been to America.'

Surprised, Susanna turned to look at Minu, and in doing so she saw the look on his father's face. A look of tension had spread across it. His lips, she noticed, had tautened into a thin, hard line, and the dark eyes were suddenly cool and expressionless.

'So you have,' he said quietly. 'But you were very young, and I am sure you cannot remember it.'

Something in the cold, still voice had its effect on Minu. He said nothing, but his eyes fell and he blushed, his pale olive skin darkening to a warm peachy tone.

Susanna felt embarrassed and bewildered, but almost before she had time to pick up her drink and take a rather nervous sip at it the moment had passed, and everything seemed normal again. A deferential waiter arrived with enormous, totally bewildering lunch menus, and as soon as the Marquis had assisted his son and his English guest to make a choice from the selection offered to them, they all moved to the big main dining-room where Susanna and her grandfather had dined with the Marquis on the night of their arrival.

Minu, obviously, was taking everything in, and as

the meal progressed his eyes seemed to grow steadily rounder. He had a healthy appetite, and having got through a generous helping of *lasagne* and a portion of salmon mayonnaise he still, apparently, had plenty of room left for the main course, which in his case took the form of hot roast chicken. But it wasn't only the food that fascinated him. It was the big, beautiful room, too, with its dazzling blue carpet and its chattering cosmopolitan clusters of brightly dressed people, and as the meal progressed his absorption became so complete that it would have seemed almost an intrusion to speak to him.

Susanna felt relaxed—far more relaxed than she would ever have expected to feel in the company of Ramiro de Säez—and also strangely, almost childishly lighthearted. Her host's rather odd, faintly chilling re-action to Minu's remark about America had evaporated quickly, and he was once again in the strangely gentle, good-humoured mood which seemed to have had him in its grip ever since they first set out that morning. Although she was very aware that on those occasions when her eyes happened to meet his there was some-thing a good deal warmer and more compelling in their dark depths than gentleness and good humour.

They sat for some time over their coffee, talking de-sultorily about Malta, and she got the impression that the Marquis was very reluctant to leave. But Minu was another matter, and despite his bubbling enthusiasm for everything around him he was still only a very small boy who simply wasn't used to so much excitement. His eyelids first began to droop noticeably about three minutes after the disappearance of his last spoonful of chocolate icecream, and soon he was swaying gently in his chair.

Susanna glanced at his father. 'I think——' she began.

'Yes.' He nodded quickly. 'We will go. At least, we will get out of here. I have to speak to my secretary about something, but you and Lor—you and Minu can wait for me in the foyer.'

With effortless ease he swung the small figure of his son up into his arms, and after wobbling uncertainly for a few seconds Minu's glossy dark head settled itself on his shoulder. Feeling half amused and half touched, Susanna realised that the august Marquis de Säez was making a serious effort to accustom himself to the use of the name Minu.

In the wide entrance hall he left them while he retired for a few minutes to his office, and Minu, having been deposited in the comfortable depths of a huge settee, immediately settled into deeper slumber. Sitting beside him, Susanna let her eyes wander casually over some of the people who were continually entering and leaving the hotel by means of the main entrance, and as she did so she suddenly caught sight of a familiar face. Or a face, at least, that she had seen before. It was Jackie Wilverton, and in almost the same instant the Australian girl recognised her.

'Well, hi!'

Jackie's sun-dress had not been cut to conceal anything that could possibly be revealed without attracting unwelcome interference from the Law, and as she crossed the reception area to speak to Susanna several pairs of dark masculine eyes followed her progress

113

with considerable interest. Days spent in the glow of the Mediterranean sun had left her skin a most attractive golden brown, and altogether she constituted a startlingly glamorous spectacle.

Moving her bag in order to make room for Jackie to sit beside her on the settee, Susanna smiled. 'How are you enjoying your holiday?' she asked.

'Oh, it's just—it's just terrific. Well, I couldn't even begin to describe ...' The big brown eyes flickered in the direction of Minu. 'What an adorable little kid! Who does he belong to? No relation of yours, is he? Not with that colouring!' Her soft, tinkling laugh reverberated around the entrance hall, and the masculine heads turned again.

'Minu is the son of the Marquis de Säez.' As she spoke the words Susanna felt a little self-conscious, and, for some reason, almost uneasy. Just as unaccountably, she felt herself flushing.

The effect on Jackie could hardly have been more explosive if she had been told that the somnolent Minu was in actual fact the heir to a prominent principality, and her whole vivid little face was transformed by a look of awed fascination. Her eyes became enormous, and when at last she spoke her voice had altered to a piercing, solemn whisper.

'Is that right?' She turned to study the small sleeping figure again, this time with appropriate respect. 'I didn't know the Marquis had any kids.'

'Minu's the only one.'

'Well, I suppose for someone like that it's important to have a son.' She stared thoughtfully at Susanna. 'You're still staying with the Marquis, then? You and

114

your grandfather, I mean?' Then she clapped a hand to her mouth. 'I'm sorry, I should have asked. How is Mr Debenham?'

'He's ... well, he's much better, thanks. The Marquis very kindly asked us both to stay with him more or less indefinitely, while my grandfather works on his new book. It's—he's made us very comfortable,' she finished rather lamely.

And at that moment she caught sight of the Marquis himself, advancing towards them across the hall. Watching him in the brief moment before his face had had time to assume a formal mask of polite recognition, she couldn't be absolutely certain whether the sight of Jackie Wilverton was a source of gratification to him or not, but he was perfectly pleasant, even charming, as he bowed slightly to the other girl. Evidently the two had bumped into each other several times since their first meeting on the dramatic night of Susanna's arrival, and Ramiro was inquiring politely whether Jackie had succeeded in running to earth a certain picturesque and secluded bathing beach which he had apparently recommended to her.

With a sudden pang—the precise nature of which she didn't feel like going into—it occurred to Susanna that she did not, after all, appear to be the only female towards whom the noble misogynist had been unbending lately. For all she knew, he and Jackie might have been dancing together almost every evening!

But the conversation between the Marquis and Jackie did not last long, and after a minute or two Jackie had said goodbye, bestowing what seemed to Susanna to be a specially intimate smile on Ramiro.

Outside in the car, he glanced round rather ruefully at Minu, now slumbering peacefully on the back seat.

'I think he has had enough—for one day, at least. We had better take him home.'

Disappointment welled up inside Susanna. She had been looking forward so much to that afternoon, but she managed somehow to hide it.

'Yes,' she said aloud, 'he's very tired. He's had quite a lot of excitement. He won't be fit for anything else today.'

There was a pause. Ramiro had fitted the key into the ignition, but he did not start the engine. 'There is no reason,' he said at last, 'why it should be the end of the day for us.' His voice was very quiet—quiet and curiously vibrant. Again he hesitated, then he turned to look at her. 'If you would have dinner with me ...'

Susanna swallowed. Then as he remained silent, she said simply: 'I'd like that.'

'Good,' he said evenly. 'I will show you Malta by night—it is a sight not to be forgotten.'

And then the engine sprang into life, and with a reckless flourish the Jaguar sped around the imposing fountain that graced the forecourt of the Grand Hotel Melita and swung out on to the road. On the back seat, Minu stirred sleepily. And all the way back along the winding coast road, driving back to the Casa, Susanna was filled with an overwhelming feeling of anticipation.

CHAPTER NINE

ROBERT DEBENHAM betrayed little outward surprise, whatever he might have felt inwardly, when he was informed that his niece would be going out for the evening with the Marquis de Säez. He was still deeply absorbed in research for his book, and as a result was spending most of his own time among Ramiro's family records.

The Marquis had suggested that they should set out at about half-past seven, and when after a lingering hour or so of preparation Susanna finally emerged from her room, the hands of the old Maltese clock at the head of the stairs had just slipped past the half hour. On her way down she dashed in hurriedly to see her grandfather, who glanced up, grunted approvingly and consented to being kissed, and then she was on her way again, speeding down the echoing stone stairs with the lightness of an errant spirit.

Outside the light was thick and golden, and the air was heavy with a drifting scent of orange-blossom from the unseen garden round the corner. Just as Susanna emerged on to the steps the sun began to sink behind the olive trees, and she noticed that the atmosphere felt warm and silky, like the waters of a carefully prepared bath. At first she was dazzled by the lowering rays of the sun, but after a moment or two, shading her eyes, she saw that the Jaguar was standing waiting for her. And beside it, resplendent in a well-cut dinner jacket, the tall figure of its owner.

As she moved towards the car she felt rather than

saw a look of admiration in his eyes, and a sudden schoolgirlish shyness made her want to avoid the odd, still intensity which she sensed in his look. She was wearing a white, diaphanous dress that clung lightly to the slender curves of her body before falling away from the hips in soft misty folds that swirled about her feet, and her bare arms and shoulders, not yet heavily tanned, looked smoothly golden.

For several seconds after she had reached him, Ramiro de Säez stood absolutely still, saying nothing. Then he seemed to come to himself, and in one swift movement he had first executed a small bow and then opened the car door for her. Daring at last to raise her eyes to his face, she realised that he was looking more handsome than she had ever seen him, and when, having settled her in his front passenger-seat, he finally got in beside her, she experienced a sudden rush of tongue-tiedness.

Reversing in a wide circle, he turned the Jaguar until its nose faced the shadowy driveway, and she saw that the sun was gone at last, swallowed up by the grey-green olive branches. A pale, misty twilight was closing in about them, and with it all the heady excitement of approaching evening.

The Marquis said very little as they made their way out through the gates and down the narrow, twisting hill road, and even when they were forced to stop for a few minutes so that a small, straggling herd of endearingly scruffy-looking goats could have a chance to edge slowly past them, he made no comment. But Susanna was enchanted by the goats, for there were some tiny white kids among them, and the kids wanted to stop and play; and she was even more enchanted by the curiously Biblical splendour of the scene spread out around her. From the place where the car had come to a halt they could look out across a wide, spreading valley—a valley over which night was falling like a soft, dark mantle—and against a luminous skyline the opposite ridge rose in jagged, rocky majesty. Everywhere, on the valley floor and on the hillsides, the little, well-tilled fields were strewn with grey-white boulders, and in the very air there was a feeling of wild and primitive closeness to the earth.

Above them, the great glimmering sky was pale and cool—and a white star, the first, hung over the faintly visible sea.

The last of the goats, skipping erratically, sidled past them, and an old man in charge of the flock came slowly behind. As he trudged by he muttered a greeting and an acknowledgment, and his dark face crinkled into a smile. He obviously knew the Marquis well.

Susanna had not asked where they were going, and her companion vouchsafed no information as they sped through the gathering darkness down from the lonely hill country and out on to a busy main road. In a curious way he seemed abstracted, and she herself felt reluctant to break the silence between them. But it was a warm, companionable silence, and it gave her no feeling of uneasiness.

At first she had assumed that they would be heading either for the Grand Hotel Melita itself—after all, when one actually owned such a magnificent establishment it might seem a little pointless to patronise one's rivals—or for one of the popular, crowded nightspots which she had heard to be found in clusters in the tourist-jammed environs of Sliema. But she soon realised that the wide highway they had joined was leading them further inland rather than towards the sea, and that they were travelling in a straight line across a broad, open plain. And then she saw the low hills rising in front of them, and she knew where they were going.

Susanna had read about Mdina, the ancient hilltop city at the heart of Malta, and she had seen photographs of it, but nothing she had read or seen had been an adequate preparation for this first view of the island's former capital. Rising against a turquoise evening sky, the old walls and towering cathedral dome had a look of fantasy and unreality, an air of belonging to some ancient, legendary world that no longer existed, and she would not have been surprised if the whole thing had suddenly disappeared from before her eyes like a mirage of the desert. It was like a fairy-tale castle, painted by some talented artist on a theatre backcloth —startlingly, romantically beautiful, but not of the real world.

Beside her, Ramiro said suddenly: 'The Silent City. There is nothing quite like it in the whole of Europe.'

Soon they had reached the foot of the hill, and then they were climbing slowly under the shadow of massive walls. The road they followed was not only steep but narrow and twisting, and Ramiro explained that it was one of the less frequented approaches. There appeared to be cultivated gardens clinging to the slopes above them, and she caught the now familiar scent of orange-blossom.

At the top they turned sharply into a huge open

space very much like an arena. The area was guarded on three sides by smooth, towering walls, and passing a line of palm trees and one or two parked cars they crossed it. On the farther side they plunged into an arched, tunnel-like passageway which led them through the thickness of the wall and out into another open space, and eventually, after a short drive through some gardens, they came to a second gateway. This, it seemed, was the entrance to Mdina proper, and when they had passed through it they emerged into a small, quiet square. Suddenly, from all sides, imposing mediaeval mansions looked down on them, and Susanna remembered what it was she had read about the Silent City—that it had been, and still was, the city of the nobles. Almost every house belonged to some ancient, titled family ... and almost every house was an architectural gem beyond price.

Slowing to a crawl, the Jaguar slipped almost soundlessly into a maze of narrow streets, and once again Susanna caught that feeling of theatrical unreality. This place was more than merely 'picturesque'. It was a thing of living beauty created long ago by men with beauty in their souls, and as they moved slowly past the silent palaces she had the strange feeling that it had not even grown old. The centuries had passed over Mdina with a touch as light as a feather, and they had left no mark.

The place they were making for turned out to be a small restaurant set high in the ramparts, and as soon as her escort had ushered her before him through the low, arched entrance, she glanced around her with delight. The walls were of natural stone, and the low, vaulted roof was supported by rows of columns, giving the place at first glance the look of a cellar. But there all resemblance to subterranean chambers ended, for on one side the long, narrow room was almost completely open to the night. Only a line of pillars, linked by rounded Norman-style arches, interposed themselves between the diners and what appeared to be the top of the old city wall, and outside, under the stars, one or two couples were already dancing to the lilting accompaniment of a small string band.

They were taken to a small table placed close by one of the outside columns, and as they sat down the Marquis glanced across at Susanna. A brief flicker of anxiety passed across his face.

'You will not be cold?' His eyes dropped to her bare shoulders.

'No.' She shook her head, her hair swinging. 'Not a bit.'

'I had forgotten that it might be a little chilly here—just yet. The evenings do not become really warm until June. With us, hot days begin in April, but even in late May it still grows cool at sunset, and we can have whole weeks of wind and rain. Summer comes slowly, and often it doesn't become established before the end of June. But ...' he smiled, 'it's worth waiting for.'

The room began to fill up. About three-quarters of their fellow diners were Maltese ... probably, Susanna decided, aristocratic Maltese. Some of the younger women were sensationally attractive, with delicate features and huge, lustrous dark eyes, and most of them, she noticed, were very skilfully made up. They tended to wear brilliant colours—the exotic, bird-ofparadise colours that suited them best—and they looked strikingly sophisticated. But despite the amount of competition present quite a few pairs of dark masculine eyes were turned in Susanna's direction, and once, after a quick look round the room, her companion glanced at her with a wry smile.

'You are attracting attention,' he told her softly. 'It is perfectly natural, but a little annoying—to me. I would prefer to have you to myself.'

She looked up, and her blue eyes, wide in the candlelight, met his softly glowing dark ones. Something in the region of her heart started jumping oddly, and she glanced down again quickly at the hors d'oeuvres with which she had been toying for the last five minutes. She was not a schoolgirl, and she had been subjected to the admiration of attractive men before, but this was something outside her experience. It was even frightening. And yet ...

'Would you like to dance?' His voice was cool and normal again, and this time she glanced up at him gratefully.

'I'd love to.'

They moved out under the stars, and as they did so the music suddenly switched from lively, throbbing rhythm to a sentimental ballad. Ramiro's arm encircled her lightly, almost casually, and she made the discovery that he was a very good dancer. She herself had always loved dancing, and she knew that they made a graceful couple. She knew, too, that other people were watching them, but it didn't worry her. Nothing worried her ... life itself was suspended, and the real world as far

123

away as the faintly glittering lights of the distant coast, just visible over the wall.

During dinner Ramiro talked a good deal, and some of the tension that had arisen between them eased again. He discussed travel with her, and as she travelled a good deal, this alone was a topic that could have carried them on almost endlessly, but from travel he turned to books, and when that subject was exhausted, to art. Very soon she discovered that they shared a passion for the elegant French school of the eighteenth century, and before long it emerged that their tastes coincided in other directions as well. For both of them Mozart and Schumann were favourite composers, and neither, it seemed, had ever been able to resist a performance of Verdi. There were so many similarities that in the end they both laughed ... and then the laughter turned once again to the kind of silence that neither of them knew quite how to handle. They danced—and this time, Susanna realised, she was held a little more closely, a little more possessively.

When they returned to their table she felt rather breathless, but Ramiro did not look at her. Instead, he glanced at his watch.

'It's rather late,' he said. His voice was gentle, even, expressionless. 'After one o'clock, as a matter of fact.'

'Oh!'

'I think perhaps we ought to be going. You'll be very tired in the morning.'

A cool, numbing flatness descended upon her. 'Yes,' she said stupidly.

Without looking at her he paid the bill, and the head waiter, bowing, ushered them out through the low doorway into the street. Behind them the door closed, and the sounds of music and murmured conversation died away. Their footsteps echoed in the empty street.

The Jaguar was parked just around the corner, and when they reached it Ramiro unlocked the doors in silence. In the shadowy, badly lit street she couldn't see his face properly, and it was impossible even to guess at what he was thinking. But as soon as they were both inside the car he turned to her and asked for the second time that evening if she were warm enough.

'I could turn the heater on . . .' He hesitated.

She shook her head. Something inside her seemed to be shivering, but it wasn't with cold. 'No, thanks.'

'It won't take long to get back.' He turned the key, and the engine sprang to life.

Beside him, Susanna sat staring through the windscreen. She felt as if he had slapped her face. What had happened? It had all been so wonderful . . . and then, in a matter of moments, the magic had gone, the golden dream had been shattered. Midnight had struck, and Cinderella, in rags, had been left alone.

A mist seemed to gather in front of her eyes. Because she couldn't help it, she sniffed, and then one large tear broke away and rolled slowly down her cheek. The next thing she knew was that the reverberations of the engine had died away again into silence, and the headlamps had been switched off. For nearly half a minute neither of them spoke. And then Ramiro got briskly out of the car and walked round to open the door for his passenger. The cool night air flooded over Susanna, and half paralysed though she was by confusion and humiliation she felt forced to look up at him. Her face seemed pale in the starlight, and her eyes were enormous.

'Come!' he said briefly. 'We will go to my house and talk.'

'Your—your house?'

'Yes.' He was looking over the top of her head, and his voice sounded clipped and cool. 'Most old Maltese families have a house in Mdina, and mine is no exception.' He glanced down at her. 'Don't be alarmed—it's perfectly respectable. I have an old housekeeper on the premises who sits up with her needlework until all hours, and if by any chance she has gone to bed she shall be roused to make coffee for us. But I have to talk to you—now.'

It passed briefly through Susanna's mind that she could easily refuse—she could, at least, make some last-minute effort to salve her pride by saying quietly and firmly that there was nothing to discuss. But even as the thought occurred to her she knew that she would do nothing of the kind. His will was too powerful ... and with a little shock she realised that even to try and maintain a pretence about her own feelings would be beyond her strength, now.

She got out of the car, and they walked in silence through the dark, cobbled alleyways of the town. There were a few lamps alight, mostly at corners and above doorways, and here and there, just above their heads, a light glowed beneath a shrine. But otherwise they were surrounded by an eerie blackness that seemed almost tangible, and Susanna knew that under any normal circumstances she would have been terrified.

But Ramiro was an expert guide, and within less

126

than five minutes they had arrived at the massive arched doorway which was the main entrance to the Palazzo de Säez. The great baroque building towered above them, shutting out the stars, and on either side she could just see, vaguely outlined, the heavy iron grilles that guarded the windows.

Her companion tugged at a sort of chain that hung beside the door, and deep in the recesses of the house a bell jangled tonelessly. In the all-pervading stillness that brooded over both the old building and the street outside the noise was an intrusion, an impertinence, and if Susanna had been alone she might have been tempted to turn and disappear into the darkness long before anyone could have time to draw back the bolts and swing the heavy oak door open. But she was not alone, and when the middle-aged housekeeper eventually materialised she returned the woman's puzzled black stare without a trace of self-consciousness. The world had turned upside down, and nothing that was happening to her now seemed quite real—possibly it was all an illusion.

Ramiro spoke rapidly in Maltese, and whatever his housekeeper's private thoughts might have been she concealed them fairly well. Her employer's unexpected arrival at half-past one in the morning, accompanied by an attractive young woman in evening dress, could hardly have failed to give her food for thought, but apart from a faint initial surprise, very little reaction showed in her face. Possibly, Susanna thought, she was used to this kind of situation—but somehow that didn't seem likely.

They moved through a vast shadowy hall dominated

by sombre-looking portraits, and into a long, opulent salon. Here again there were portraits, and a good deal of heavy Italian furniture. It was rather stuffy in the room, and the housekeeper opened some of the windows, and threw back the faded green shutters. A breeze began to stir the curtains, and with it, from the unseen gardens, came the faint scent of dew and oleanders.

'Well, sit down.' From his manner, the Marquis could have been a lawyer receiving a rather troublesome client, and his cool, highly civilised detachment should have been more than enough to dispel any uneasiness on Susanna's part. 'In a few minutes Josette will bring us coffee, and then ... then there is something I have to explain to you.'

Susanna had subsided slowly on to a rather uncomfortable brocade-covered chair. She looked small and insubstantial in the drifting white dress, and there was an unaccustomed air of childlike bewilderment about her. Ramiro turned his eyes away from her, and without glancing in her direction again indicated the handsome rosewood piano at the far end of the room.

'You play, don't you? I would ... like to hear those keys brought to life again. My father brought that particular instrument back from Vienna.'

She didn't feel like playing the piano. In fact, she had never felt less like doing anything, and for a moment she stared at him uncomprehendingly. But then, as if in obedience to a hypnotist, she rose and moved slowly down the length of the room. The great, gleaming grand piano was unlocked, and beside it on a low table there was a stack of worn sheet music. On top of the pile lay a book of Beethoven sonatas, and she opened it at random. *Sonata Pathétique* ... That, she thought with detachment, should suit her mood.

The first notes stole on to the quiet air a little hesitantly, for she had not played for some time, but she played with natural sensitivity. After a time, too, the soothing quality of the music began to have its effect on her, and some of the tension and bewilderment she had been feeling drained away. The sonata gave place to a nocturne by Chopin, and then to a sad, gentle Schubert waltz. She didn't hear Josette return with the coffee, and she didn't hear her leave again, closing the door quietly behind her. It was only when Ramiro de Säez came to stand behind her that her consciousness was penetrated, and then a little warm glow of awareness spread through her. She had just embarked on the rippling loveliness of Schumann's *Devotion*—a piece which they had agreed earlier was a favourite with both of them—but his nearness unnerved her, and her fingers hesitated on the keys.

'Please go on.'

He had moved forward a little, and as if under some sort of compulsion Susanna looked up at him. She was pale, and she had a feeling of uncertainty. His eyes were unfathomable, but at the same time something in their depths made her look away quickly. Her hands dropped to her lap, and she stood up.

'I—I'm boring you ...'

But even as the words were uttered she felt her eyes drawn back to him, and this time—this time there was no escape. His dark, mesmeric gaze was engulfing her

... something seemed to be spinning inside her head, and the room wavered.

He took one swift, soundless step towards her, and the next second she was in his arms, held in a possessive, vice-like grip that threatened to crush her ribs. If she had wanted to struggle it would have been pointless, but somehow the idea of resistance—even a token resistance—didn't enter her head. This was what she had been born for, this was where she belonged—in the strong and infinitely comforting circle of Ramiro's arms. And there was a kind of exquisite relief in feeling that she had come home at last.

'Susanna ...' His voice was strange and husky, hardly recognisable, and there was an odd note of ragged desperation about it. His left hand tugged gently at her hair, and her head tilted back. 'Darling —my darling ...'

And then their lips met, and Susanna was caught up in waves of ecstasy that seemed almost to rob her of consciousness. The kiss went on for a long time, and when it ended she was trembling violently. He kissed her eyelids and her ears and the top of her head, and then he lifted her slight, unresisting body and carried her over to one of the big, damask-covered armchairs. Still holding her, he sat down, and any faint stirrings of reason that might have been beginning to penetrate her bewildered senses went out of the window as soon as he looked once again into her eyes.

She had no will ... no past and no future. And no wishes that were not connected with him.

'Tell me you're real,' he whispered suddenly. He bent his lips to her throat. 'Tell me you're not a sprite

130

or a nymph ... that you won't leave me.'

Her cheek against his, she stirred slightly. When she spoke her voice was husky with the wonder of self-giving.

'I'll never leave you,' she promised. How could he think she would? 'I—I belong to you. I always will. Oh ... Ramiro, I love you so much more than anything in the world—much more than my own life!'

There was silence. He lifted his head, but it was several seconds before she realised that his hold on her was slowly but surely relaxing. Almost imperceptibly, he seemed to detach himself from her, and then, suddenly, with cruel, dispassionate finality, he set her on her feet and stood up. Somewhere, far off in the house, a clock chimed two.

'I'm sorry,' he said. His voice, like the silvery chimes of the clock, seemed to come from a very long way away. He didn't look at her. 'That's all I can say.'

Susanna stood very still. At last, from between dry lips, her voice sounded quietly and clearly. 'I ... don't understand.'

He looked at her then, and the flash of cold anger in his eyes almost caused her to shrink.

'Don't you? Then I had better explain.' His accent had become very noticeable, and the words seemed to be ground out between his teeth. 'I don't want your undying love ... I don't want your love at all!'

This time she did shrink. One of her hands had been resting on the back of a Louis Quinze chair, and her delicately pointed nails dug fiercely into the inlaid wood.

Ramiro de Säez walked to the door and swung it

131

wide. Then he turned to stare at her. Everything about him seemed to have changed.

'You're not a sheltered Maltese girl, and you are no longer in your teens. You seem quite sophisticated, and though I realise that is probably an erroneous impression, this is, after all, the second half of the twentieth century. I naturally assumed you would understand the sort of—interlude I had in mind. It could have been quite amusing for both of us.'

When he had finished speaking there was a long, heavy silence that pressed on Susanna's ear-drums. She felt strangely cold, and she knew that if she didn't move quickly she would not be able to move at all. Without looking at Ramiro, she walked out through the open door, and after a moment or two he followed her.

CHAPTER TEN

AFTERWARDS, Susanna remembered hardly anything of that long, silent drive back to the Casa de Säez. She knew that she felt very cold, and that at the same time her whole body was damp with perspiration. And she knew that Ramiro de Säez stared at the road before him without once turning his head. But apart from that the whole thing was a blank in her memory—a merciful blank.

She did, however, remember parting from Ramiro in the hall of the Casa. He did not look at her, but just as she reached the foot of the stairs he spoke, causing her to stop in her tracks.

'Susanna ...! I could call you Miss Baird, but perhaps for the time being we'll stick to "Susanna".'

She turned slowly, a look of puzzled, detached inquiry in her face.

'You must listen to me, just for a moment.' His voice was clipped and strained. 'I want your grandfather to remain here as my guest—I intend him to remain, until he has finished his book. You should not need to be told how important it is to him. But if he is to stay, you must stay also.' He paused. 'You have my apologies for what happened tonight. It will not be repeated.'

She said nothing, and he went on.

'Tomorrow morning I'll go over to the Melita, and I shall remain there for several days. When I return here perhaps we shall at least be able to treat each other with reasonable civility. Don't worry, I'll make certain that you see as little of me as possible.' Another pause. 'Within a fortnight I shall be going abroad on business, and I may not be back until the autumn. I shall leave this house at your disposal, and I hope that you—that your grandfather will make use of it for as long as it appeals to him.' He moved towards one of the doors on the left of the hall. 'Goodnight,' he said abruptly. And then he was gone.

For several seconds after he had disappeared, Susanna stood quite still. And then, rather slowly, she began to climb the stairs. Back in the security of her own room, she knelt in front of the open window and rested her head in her hands. A night breeze lifted the ends of her hair and far below, in the dark, sequestered garden, the olive branches rustled.

Her numbed brain cleared a little, and the thought

occurred to her that she had to get away. How could she possibly stay in his house ... how could she? How could she stand the daily agony of contact with his home, his possessions—even, of occasional contact with him?

But then she thought of her grandfather, sleeping soundly in another part of the house, and of his intense, almost childlike pleasure in his work. Living in this place, studying the ancient books and records that were so important for his research, he was completely happy. Could she ask him to leave it all, almost before he had started—and in any case, would he? A little wryly, she admitted to herself that he probably would not.

Some time later she took her clothes off and lay down on the bed. She had made up her mind that she would have to stay. And when at long last, somewhere near dawn, her eyelids drooped and sleep closed in on her, one clear thought ran through her mind. Staying near Ramiro might mean pain and bitter unhappiness ... but going away from everything connected with him—that would be more than she could bear.

It was late when she awoke—almost ten o'clock—and the room was warm with sunshine. Carmen, who knew she had been out the evening before, was just coming in with her breakfast-tray, and the Maltese woman's face was wreathed in smiles.

'You eat, then sleep again,' she recommended cheerfully. Coyly, she added: 'Is-Signur went out very early. He went to Melita Hotel.' It was quite obvious that she thought this would be sufficient reason for Susanna not to hurry up.

134

When she had gone Susanna leant back against her pillows. Memory was flooding back over her, and as it did so it seemed as if her whole body began to ache. But after a minute or two she forced herself to drink a cup of coffee, and then, slowly, she dressed.

Later in the morning she went to see her grandfather. He was surrounded by books, and he looked as relaxed as a contented, well-cared-for cat. Making a tremendous effort she smiled at him brightly, and then curled up in a chair near his own.

'Enjoying yourself?' she asked lightly.

He looked up, his eyes keen beneath the shaggy brows. She knew at once that something in her face caught his attention, and it was a relief when his scrutiny came to an end. Frowning slightly, he turned back to his papers.

'I nearly always enjoy myself.' With great care, he closed a heavy morocco-bound book, and laid it aside. 'Well, how did the Ogre make out as an escort?'

There was a tiny pause.

'He was charming.' At least her voice wasn't going to let her down. 'We went to Mdina.'

'Ah!' His brows lifted a little. 'Delightful idea. Whereabouts in Mdina?'

'A sort of night-club—high up in the ramparts. I—I don't remember the name of the place, but it was nice ... great fun.' Unable to stand the strain any longer, she got up and moved away, pretending to be interested in the stacks of books that surrounded her grandfather. Casually, she picked one up. 'What's this? *Private Lives of the Great Maltese Families*. Sixteenth-century scandal?'

He glanced at the volume in question. 'Partly. Sue——'

'Yes, Grandpapa?' Her whole body tensed. He had not been distracted, that was obvious. He was still thinking about her excursion of the evening before, and her too-brief description had not satisfied him. She waited, holding her breath. Somehow, she would have to parry any awkward questions.

But they didn't come. Whether or not the wariness in her voice had acted as a hint she couldn't be sure, but there was silence for over a minute. Then he said:

'Hand me a pen, will you? There's one on the desk, over there.'

She obeyed, and he took it from her without looking up. Once again he seemed absorbed in his work, and he began to make a series of notes. A little while later he recollected her presence.

'Well, Sue, you can run along now. I won't be downstairs for lunch; but I'll see you this evening.'

It was his usual way of dismissing her, and it probably meant that he wanted to concentrate. She felt almost weak with relief, and a little upsurge of gratitude made her go across to him and put an arm round his shoulders.

'You're sure you don't want me to take dictation?' It would give her something to do, and through the haze of her own unhappiness she felt rather guilty about her grandfather.

'Not yet, I'm not ready. Go along now ... take yourself for a drive, or amuse the brat for a while.'

Outside his door, she stood still. She had a dull, insistent headache, and she knew that more than any-

thing else she would like to go and lie down for a while.
But she also knew that if she did so she would be left
alone with her thoughts, and that ... that would definitely not be a good idea. Also, she supposed she ought
to go and see Minu. The thought of Minu hurt like
the cold, sharp jab of a needle—just as everything connected with his father would always hurt her—but that
wasn't important. He couldn't be neglected, and
though he had been too tired and contented to mind
being brought home early the day before, he might begin to feel unwanted if he were left alone today.

It was not until she had already opened the door of
the day nursery that she remembered Brother Bernard
and the morning lessons—something she would not
normally have forgotten—and by that time it was too
late to draw back. The little monk had already risen,
beaming, and when she tried to protest that she didn't
want to interrupt anything, he shook his head emphatically.

'No, no, you are not interrupting anything! We have
just finished our mathematics lesson, and I think we
shall both be glad of a rest. Don't you think so, Minu?'
His round brown eyes twinkled, and Minu, who had
been hesitating dutifully before laying down his pencil, abandoned it with a clatter and rushed awkwardly
across the room to fling his arms around Susanna.
Simba and Julian had been lying near him, and they,
too, got up and came to greet her, their slender tails
waving.

Startled and a little taken aback by this reception,
she hugged Minu and patted each of the dogs in turn.
Then she looked at Brother Bernard. They had met

137

once before, and she had taken a liking to the kindly, sensible Franciscan. For a long time, she suspected, he had probably been the brightest influence in Minu's life, and it was obvious that the child was very fond of him.

'I'm so sorry,' she told him. 'I should have remembered you'd be busy.'

'It's all right, it's all right.' He looked indulgently at Minu, and put out a square, work-roughened hand to ruffle his hair. 'Go and find the work you have been doing on your geography project. Then Miss Susanna will be able to see that there is something—just a little —inside this head after all.'

Minu limped slowly away to search through a cupboard on the other side of the room, and Brother Bernard looked at Susanna. It was a searching, quizzical look, and it made her feel faintly uncomfortable.

'You are fond of the child?' It was a statement rather than a question, but it seemed to require an answer.

'Yes. Yes, I'm ... very fond of him.'

'He is attached to you. Children of his age——' The friar's eyes travelled to where Minu was still rummaging through the cupboard, and for a moment he hesitated. Then he went on: 'Any child of his age needs a feminine influence. The most important person—the most important thing in a child's life is his mother. And if, tragically, something happens to the mother ...' An expressive shrug. 'Then a substitute should be found. Sometimes a man who has lost his wife may not wish to remarry, but if he is left with young children I believe he should not hesitate.' Brother Bernard's shrewd gaze fastened itself firmly upon Susanna. 'Don't you agree?' he asked.

But at that moment Minu came across to them with the results of his labours in the field of geography, and she was spared the necessity of answering. Instead, she was able to devote all her energies to admiring the 'project', which turned out to be quite a detailed study of South America. All the countries in the area had been described, their principal crops and industries listed and their highest mountains and longest rivers carefully enumerated. An impressive map had been drawn up, and although one or two of the national boundary lines seemed to bulge in some surprising places, and Brazil appeared to be a good deal smaller than Peru, it was nevertheless quite an achievement for a nine-year-old. Undoubtedly Minu was bright. She was lavish with her praise, and he flushed with pleasure. Brother Bernard, too, was gratified, for he was proud of his pupil, and it was some time before the subject of the project was exhausted. By the time it had been examined in every detail the hands of the large nursery clock had moved well past twelve, and Susanna had an excellent excuse for taking her departure. Nursery lunch, she knew, was served at half-past twelve, and Brother Bernard would be sharing it with his charge.

Extricating herself at last, she left them preparing their books for the afternoon's theological studies, and a little while later she went downstairs, to lunch alone in the long, cool dining-room at the back of the house. Her grandfather was in his room, and once again Marthese de Säez had gone out to visit a relative. She herself would have given anything for a chance to skip the meal—which threatened to choke her—but Carmen, she knew, would not have allowed that.

After lunch she wrote some letters, and then attempted to get to grips with a recently published novel which she had been meaning to read ever since leaving England. The novel dragged and after a time she abandoned it, but somehow or other she got through the rest of the day. Then, almost before she knew it, it was evening, and having dressed very simply in a long skirt and silky, cream-coloured top she went downstairs to the *salotto*.

Her grandfather was there, and so was Marthese. To her surprise they were in the middle of quite an animated conversation, and a lot of the Maltese woman's shyness seemed to have evaporated. They were discussing local customs, and Marthese was clearly turning out to be very informative. To Susanna's infinite relief they talked throughout the whole of dinner, and she was allowed to get away with contributing nothing more than an occasional word. She had always known that her grandfather could be charming, but she had never known him exert himself so consistently to be pleasant and approachable, and she wondered what it was about the Signurina de Säez that interested him.

People were strange, and friendship was strange—and love was strange. She began to feel a little dizzy, and decided to go to bed early. No one attempted to detain her, and when she left the *salotto*, a little after nine o'clock, Robert Debenham and Marthese de Säez were getting on better than ever. They had just discovered that they both played chess.

Alone in her own room, Susanna undressed and got into bed. Neither her grandfather nor the Signurina had commented on Ramiro's absence ... but she had thought of little else throughout the evening.

The following morning was very warm but overcast and steamy, with almost a hint of rain in the air. According to Carmen rain was unlikely, for in Malta the weather between May and September is almost completely dry, and they were already into June. But there was no denying that it was rather cloudy, and Susanna felt an odd sort of relief. Grey, hazy weather suited her mood better than the unvarying sunshine of the last few days.

After breakfast she felt restless, and as soon as she had made sure that her grandfather didn't need her she set out to walk the half-mile or so to the beach at the end of the valley. The fairly strenuous exercise was a relief, and by the time she reached the tiny, sandy cove some of the tautness seemed to have gone out of her. It was warm and very still in the shelter of the rocky cliffs, and only the faintest hint of a breeze whispered across the glassy surface of the sea. Feeling oddly limp, she perched herself on a rock and sat staring at the small, rippling waves.

Throughout the previous day she had hardly allowed herself to think. Somewhere, she knew, locked away in the depths of her being, there was more pain and humiliation than she dared face up to, and for that reason she had been afraid even to go over what had happened in her own mind. She had felt numbed, almost as if she had been given an anaesthetic, and to a certain extent that numbness was still with her. But now, as she sat on the lonely rock gazing out to sea, an aching, suffocating misery began to creep over her, and for the first time she started to wonder why it had to happen.

The one thing she was certain of was the fact that she still loved Ramiro—and that she always would love him. She, who never before in her life had felt more than moderately attracted to any man ... For Ramiro St Vincent de Säez she knew that she would give up everything. Everything that had ever mattered in her life.

She could not have prevented herself falling in love with Ramiro, she was sure of that. But why had he treated her as he had done? He had carried her with him towards a peak of undreamed-of happiness, and then ... And then he had let her fall with such strange, brutal callousness that she would bear the scars of that bitter rejection for the rest of her life. Undoubtedly the tragic loss of Minu's mother had done something terrible to him. But, however much he had loved his wife, did he have to punish every other woman because Célèstine was dead?

For a few brief, wonderful moments it had seemed as if what was happening between them might be as important for him as it certainly was for her, and during those moments he had said: 'Tell me you won't leave me'. Why had he said that? And why, just because she had told him the truth about her own feelings —how the humiliation of it stung!—had everything been shattered in an instant?

What had he thought she was demanding—expecting of him? However little he might have been prepared to offer her she would have taken it gladly, and something like a quiver of fear ran through her as, for the first time, she faced up to the fact.

'Break, break, break, on thy cold gray stones, O Sea! ... And I would that my tongue could utter the thoughts that arise in me!'

The quiet voice behind her made her jump and swing round—and then she saw Peter Hamblyn, just sliding on to the rock beside her.

'A penny for them,' he said lightly, smiling into her startled face. 'Of course, if you're just thinking that you can't stand Tennyson I'll switch poets. The old boy tends to be frowned on these days, mainly because he liked things to rhyme. But his rhymes didn't stop him making some pretty profound comments on the human condition ... Don't you agree?'

Feeling like someone abruptly awakened from a confused dream, Susanna stared at him.

'Look, I'm sorry,' he said quickly. 'I mean, if I startled you. I didn't realise you were so completely lost. Shall I go away?'

Struggling up through the mists of her own self-absorption, she shook her head. It was a relief to have to talk.

'No, of course not. You took me by surprise, that's all. You were quoting Tennyson, weren't you?'

'Yes, but never mind. Listen, I've just been talking to your grandfather. That's to say, I was twenty minutes ago. He and I have fixed something up for to-morrow, and we were wondering if you would join us. I was wondering, that is—and hoping. Your grandfather seems pretty sure you'll fall in obediently, whatever he asks you to do.'

She forced a smile. 'What is it you've been planning?'

'Just a little trip around some of the old monuments—places of archaeological interest. I know your grandfather hasn't been going about much, but apparently he's ready to come up for air, now. And he particularly wants to do this.'

'Yes, I know. He's been doing some very solid research work, but he told me the other day that he'd soon be ready to get out and about the Island. He just wanted to do some intensive reading about everything before seeing things for himself.'

'Well, he's all set now, and we're planning to make a day of it. You'll come, won't you?' he said pleadingly. 'The Signurina de Säez is coming—your grandfather's charm seems to have had quite an effect on her! So you could say we'll make a foursome.'

'It sounds fun.' She made a determined effort to sound enthusiastic. 'Of course I'll come. When do we set out? Early tomorrow morning?'

'Yes, the earlier the better, I should think. The midday heat isn't unbearable yet, but the first part of the morning is certainly the pleasantest and it would be a pity to waste it. By the way, you don't need to bring a car. Mine will easily hold all four of us.'

Soon afterwards, Peter set out to return to the Villa Célèstine, and Susanna, finding it was later than she'd realised, started back through the valley. She was glad about the excursion that had been planned for the following day. At least it would be something to do, and also it meant an opportunity to get away—if only for a few hours—from the Casa de Säez. As for Peter Hamblyn ... well, if he simply wanted to be friends it was all right. If he wanted something more—and she had a feeling he did—she would just have to make him understand, as quickly as possible, that she wasn't for him.

Suddenly, she knew far too much about being hurt to want the same fate inflicted on anybody else.

Soon after eight o'clock the following morning Peter turned up, driving a smart cream-coloured Rover which he had brought with him from England. Everybody was ready to set out, and well before nine they were on the road. The morning was fresh and sparkling, blue and gold, and the excellent spirits of the driver seemed to communicate themselves to at least two of his passengers. Robert Debenham, installed in the front passenger seat, was relaxed and almost exuberant, and the change in Marthese de Säez was surprising. Her face was softened and eager, alight with anticipation, and the well-cut linen dress she was wearing took at least ten years off her age. It wasn't difficult to assess how much of this transformation was due to the consistent attention being paid her by her nephew's English guest, and Susanna, noticing, felt faintly worried. Marthese mustn't get the wrong impression ... her grandfather, once he really put himself out to be charming, could be nothing short of a menace to susceptible middle-aged ladies. It was one thing to be kind, but—well, she would have to speak to him.

Apart from this, though, Susanna noticed very little. She left comment and conversation mainly to the other three, willing them to leave her alone, and although she had an uneasy feeling that Peter's attention rarely wandered away from her for long, he didn't bother her.

The drive turned out to be very pleasant—or, at least, she would normally have found it pleasant—and some of the things they saw were tremendously interesting. There were the prehistoric temples, rather similar to Stonehenge but smaller and differently planned, the only examples of their kind in the world and of absorbing interest to archaeologists. Robert Debenham, darting about the massive ruins like a child in a sweet-shop, announced that he was enjoying one of the most fascinating experiences of his life, and for his benefit Marthese eagerly recounted her childhood memories of visiting the ruins. Leaving the temples, they visited some fine Roman baths, and then went on to inspect the foundations of the house once occupied by St Publius, the Roman who had been Governor of the Island in the time of St Paul, and who had become the Apostle's first convert in Malta.

They stopped for lunch at a pleasant restaurant situated at the southern tip of the Island, close by the sea, and once again Susanna became conscious of the fact that Peter Hamblyn rarely seemed to forget her for an instant. Often she looked up to find his eyes upon her, and she couldn't help realising that he did everything possible to ensure that she was comfortable, and that she enjoyed herself.

After lunch they visited more temples, an underground grotto with a fascinating echo, and the cata-

146

combs of the early Christians—which were located in Rabat, very close to Mdina. Looking across at the old city, Susana felt a bitter twinge at the memories it invoked, and instantly she found Peter beside her.

'Got a headache?' he asked, studying her face shrewdly.

'No.' She smiled at him. 'I think I'm just feeling the heat.'

'I'm not surprised. Do we all go out to dinner tonight, or are you too worn out?'

'I'd rather go back early, if you don't mind. But ask the others; perhaps you three could go somewhere.'

'Without you?' He raised one eyebrow in a quizzical smile which she might have found fascinating if she had not been so completely immunised against the attractions of all men but one. 'I could think of things I'd rather do. Your grandfather can take the Signurina de Säez out for a gay evening if he likes, but if you're not going then neither am I. Susanna——' She had let herself drop wearily on to a low stone wall, and he sat down beside her. 'Susanna, won't you let me take you out one evening? Just as a friend?'

She looked away from him, and her eyes wandered unseeingly over the shimmering evening landscape spread out below them.

'Peter, I don't feel like going out at all just now— not with anyone. That's the truth.'

'Well, I don't have to have it spelt out for me that it's not just because of your grandfather.' There was a pause, and then he glanced again at her averted head. 'I know I shouldn't ask, but is it someone you met out here?'

She stood up abruptly. 'It doesn't really matter, does it? Look, the others are waiting for us. We'd better go back to them.'

It was dusk by the time Peter returned them to the Casa de Säez. With scarcely a sound the long white car pulled up before the front door, and Susanna climbed out. Behind her, Robert Debenham and Marthese de Säez were talking and laughing about something, and Peter was caught up with them. Feeling tired and flat, she moved away a little into the warm, moth-laden twilight and stood gazing over the low wall into the garden at the side of the house. And then she caught the sound of voices—a man's voice, and a child's. They came closer, and she heard the sound of footsteps approaching.

Seconds later, Ramiro de Säez appeared on the other side of the iron gate ... and with him were Minu and the two dogs.

Susanna felt tied to the spot. For just an instant they stared at one another—and then the gate was open, and Minu was hurling himself at her, exactly as he had done the day before in the nursery. His rather spindly arms hugged her convulsively, and his small dark head pressed itself hard against her.

'I wondered where you were!' His tone was reproachful, and so, when he flung his head back to look up at her, were his great dark eyes.

'I went out for the day, darling.' She spoke automatically, shocked by the fact that he had evidently been upset. 'Your Aunt Marthese went too, and so did my grandfather. Mr—Mr Hamblyn took us.'

148

'I see.' This time it was the man who spoke, and his voice was disapproving.

Determinedly, Susanna kept her eyes on Minu. 'Didn't Carmen tell you?' she asked. 'We would have taken you, Minu, but you wouldn't have liked it, really. You'd have been bored, and it would have tired you out, too.' She knelt down, gazing anxiously into his quivering, half-averted face. 'We'll go out tomorrow,' she promised desperately. 'Just you and I ... we'll go anywhere you like.'

He shook his head slowly. 'I can't go tomorrow. I have to do an examination.' But his face had brightened.

'The next day, then, or as soon as Brother Bernard will let you. That's a promise!'

'I'm afraid it can't be.' Ramiro de Säez had come up to them, and his voice sounded quiet and incisive on the evening air. 'In the autumn Minu will be beginning his serious education, and during the next few days I shall be taking him to visit some suitable schools. I never know in advance exactly when I am going to be free, so he must be available to go with me at any time.'

'I ... understand.' Slowly, she straightened up, a vivid flush staining her cheeks. But the flush faded as quickly as it had come, and her voice was detached as she added: 'I'm sorry. I didn't mean to interfere with your arrangements.'

'I'm sure you didn't.' But his tone was sceptical. And then he turned his head to take in the group still gathered around the car. 'You have had a pleasant day?' he inquired politely.

'Yes. It was very interesting.' Whatever happened,

the unhappiness inside her must not show in her voice. 'We saw the Catacombs, and—and the temple at Tarxien ...' Under his coldly critical gaze her throat contracted, and she fumbled for words. 'We saw ... excavations ...'

And then Peter Hamblyn appeared behind her, and she was spared the necessity of saying anything more.

'Sorry I absconded with your house-guests!' Peter's tone was casual and pleasant. 'But Mr Debenham suddenly felt like emerging from seclusion, and he wanted to take a look at some historic places. Your aunt agreed to come along too, and so did Susanna.' He glanced at the girl beside him, and there was no doubt about the sudden softening in his eyes and voice.

'I am delighted that you have all been passing your time so ... profitably.' The Marquis's tone was light and urbane, but the look in his eyes was the very opposite. Was he jealous? Susanna wondered. She could almost have sworn that he was, and something within her lifted a little. But the next instant the impression vanished, and she decided it had been an illusion.

He was still addressing Peter. 'I hope you'll go inside for a drink. Unfortunately I shan't be able to join you, as I'm already late for a dinner engagement.' And then he turned to Susanna, and this time there was nothing at all to be discovered from the look in his eyes. 'You must go out more often,' he remarked. His tone was pleasant, almost kindly. 'There is still so much that you ought to see before you leave Malta. And if Mr Hamblyn has the time ...' his detached glance shifted to include the other man, 'I'm sure you could not find a more suitable escort.'

Ramiro de Säez turned away, and automatically Susanna walked back towards the front door, Peter Hamblyn at her side. But although he spoke to her, she didn't hear a word.

CHAPTER ELEVEN

ONE by one, the June days passed. It grew hotter, and as temperatures soared Susanna came to appreciate the airy coolness of the Casa de Säez. Old stone walls, she found, kept merciless heat at bay more effectively than many of the modern inventions specially designed to cope with it, and Carmen's skilful adjustment of windows and shutters ensured that glare was kept to a minimum. Since the owner of the house disliked air-conditioning this had never been installed, but there were highly efficient electric fans in every room, and small, soundless gadgets fitted high in the walls made certain that flies and mosquitoes were never seen.

Susanna lived each day as it came, not looking ahead and trying, as far as possible, not to look back. Her grandfather's book made smooth and rapid progress, and she spent a lot of time helping him with it. Not only was there a vast amount of typing to be done but he liked to discuss his work with her, and because she needed something that would occupy her thoughts exclusively she threw herself into the task with all the energy of which she was capable. She had always done her best to help her grandfather when he was working, but this was different. Never before had she needed desperately to forget everything else. The book took shape as a historical novel of compelling power.

As soon as Ramiro de Säez had taken Minu to see various schools he left for Sicily, and there, as week followed week, he remained. In accordance with her promise Susanna took Minu out, not once but several times, and when she was not with her grandfather she seemed to spend most of her time with the small, dark-haired boy. They usually went to secluded beaches, where she could swim and Minu could paddle—his twisted foot made swimming dangerous—and sometimes they picnicked in the inadequate shadow of a sun-umbrella brought from the house. Minu grew brown and healthy-looking, and his confidence in himself and in life seemed to increase every day. Susanna became deeply fond of him, and she knew that he was almost as attached to her ... too attached, she sometimes thought. What was going to happen when, quite soon now, she went out of his life for good? He might feel abandoned, betrayed, and it could upset him badly. When she was with him she tried not to think of his father, but it wasn't easy. And besides, Minu often wanted to talk about the parent with whom he had only just begun to establish a happy and satisfactory relationship.

Susanna found that summer, in Malta, was a time for parties, outings and endless relaxation ... for one thing, a lighthearted and casual approach to life made the temperature easier to bear. But she clung to her determination to avoid social contacts, and Peter Hamblyn, telephoning regularly, found her resolution impossible to shake.

Then, one evening, the telephone rang just as she and Minu were coming in from the garden. It was actually past Minu's bedtime, but they had found one of the hedgehogs—Minu said it was Giuza—swimming in the goldfish pond, and as it couldn't get out they had had to go to its assistance. Fortunately it had turned out to be co-operative, and Susanna, to the delight of her companion, had lifted it out with the aid of a small trowel. Shaking itself, it had hurried off into the bushes, and they walked back slowly through the orange grove—or Susanna walked back slowly, while Minu made his way energetically from tree to tree for the purpose of inspecting the young fruit.

It was the last night of June, and the sky was already a misty blaze of stars, very high and very bright. In Susanna's nostrils there was a scent of roses and warm earth, and the air was soft as velvet. Somewhere, beyond the fields, a dog barked, and then there was a muffled booming sound as an early firework exploded over the village of Mgarr. She had grown accustomed, now, to the sound of fireworks. Every week during the summer months, she had discovered, some town or village in Malta had its *festa*—and a *festa* meant fireworks. This week, she supposed, it must be the turn of Mgarr.

She stood still beneath a large, leafy orange tree, inhaling the beauty of the night. And as she did so something seemed to catch at her heartstrings. Pain and loneliness swept over her. For the first time in weeks, tears stung behind her eyelids, and frightened by the bleakness of her own thoughts, she hurried on towards the house, calling to Minu to follow her.

153

It was just as they reached the house that the telephone rang. It was Carmen's evening off, and after hesitating for only a moment Susanna sent Minu upstairs and answered it herself. It was Peter Hamblyn.

'Hello.' As always, his voice was a little tense. 'How's life in the convent?'

She forced herself to sound light and casual. 'About the same as usual. How's the outside world?'

'Not inspiring. Look—Susanna, you're fond of music, aren't you? Well, there's something rather special coming on at the Manoel. Some top Italian company is doing *Madam Butterfly*, and—are you listening?'

'Yes, of course I'm listening.'

'I've got two tickets, and—look, for heaven's sake, you've got to come with me. You can't stay shut up there for ever. Unless ...' His voice altered. 'Unless, of course, you're not shut up there any more. Maybe there's someone who is luckier than I am.'

'There isn't,' she assured him.

'Then—honestly, I know you'd love this, and there's no earthly reason why you shouldn't come.' He stopped. 'Susanna, I'm not asking so very much.'

She closed her eyes, passing her free hand across them wearily. With the other she took a firmer grip of the receiver. Rationality ... She must be rational.

'It's nice of you to ask me.' Her voice sounded perfectly normal. 'I—I like Puccini. Thanks, Peter, I'd love to go with you.'

She heard the sharp intake of his breath. There was silence for about five seconds, and when he spoke his voice was slightly husky. 'Good girl,' he said softly.

The performance was scheduled to begin at half-past seven in the evening, and it was just after six on the following Tuesday when Peter's cream-coloured car nosed its way along the drive to the Casa de Säez. Susanna had not yet made her appearance downstairs, but Robert Debenham was relaxing in a basket-chair on the terrace at the back of the house, and the visitor was taken out to join him. The sun was still fairly high in the western sky, but from five o'clock onwards the terrace was in shadow, and there was even the faint suspicion of a breeze from the sea. Since the worst of the heat was past for another day both men drank whisky, and as they talked the sky grew paler and the brilliance and the light began to fade.

Just before half-past six Susanna appeared behind them, and she didn't miss the look that sprang into Peter's eyes as he rose swiftly to his feet. She wished she could have missed it. She had dressed carefully because she didn't want to let him down—she had taken more trouble with her appearance than she had taken for a long time, but she hadn't meant to provoke—well, not quite that kind of look. Her long, floating skirt was of a pale mint green, and with it she wore a white top lightly embroidered with silver thread. At one time she had thought of lifting the bright swathe of her hair into a coil on top of her head—as she often did when she was in England—but then she had realised that on a Maltese July evening the weight of it would be unbearable, and it lay on her shoulders in a thick, shimmering cloak.

The Manoel Theatre turned out to be situated in one of the oldest and narrowest streets at the heart of

Valletta, and parking outside the building—or anywhere near, for that matter—was out of the question. So they left the car in a little square dominated by the graceful shape of St Paul's Anglican Cathedral, and made their way on foot to the theatre.

The street outside was crowded with people in evening dress who had arrived early and were determined to linger as long as possible in the relatively fresh evening air, and more were being disgorged every minute from cars that stopped as briefly as the drivers could manage before moving on again up the narrow street. Several police were on duty, for the President of the Island was expected, and there was a feeling of pleasant anticipation in the air. Susanna and her escort stood for a few minutes watching the crowds, and then they moved into the even denser mass of humanity that packed the foyer.

Peter put a hand beneath her arm. 'Let's go straight in and look at the auditorium. It's worth studying.'

The heart of the little theatre was still almost empty, and they were able to stand in silence and gaze around them at the lovely tiers of boxes and the delicate beauty of the painted ceiling. It was said, Susanna knew, to be the oldest theatre in Europe, but its atmosphere was overwhelmingly of the eighteenth century. It seemed built for performances of Haydn and Mozart, and she felt that if one were alone in the place it might be almost frighteningly easy to imagine it peopled with ladies in hooped gowns and gentlemen in powdered wigs.

Peter had succeeded in securing a box, and a short time later they went up to it. Gradually the auditorium filled up, and then casually and without hurry, in the Maltese way, the Manoel Theatre Orchestra started to assemble below the stage. There was a murmur of many voices, and Susanna recognised snatches not only of English and Maltese but of French, German and Italian as well. She leaned forward, looking over the edge of the box, and saw that the audience was, for the most part, strikingly well dressed. English and Continental visitors, as well as the Maltese themselves, seemed to have gone to real trouble to make themselves presentable for the occasion, and it was a glittering, romantic scene. The neighbouring boxes, she noticed, were mostly occupied by aristocratic Maltese, and the same applied to those opposite. There were one or two interesting combinations, though ... In one of the boxes on a level with their own a very pretty blonde girl had just come in with a dark-haired man. There was, Susanna thought vaguely, something faintly familiar about the girl, but the man was still half-hidden in the shadows at the back of the box.

And then he came forward. The orchestra struck up the overture, and he sat down in the full glare of the lights. It was the Marquis St Vincent de Säez ... And beside him, sparkling and beautiful, was Jackie Wilverton.

The overture came to an end and the curtain rose. All the lights went down. Pulses thundered in Susanna's ears and her hands felt cold and clammy. She must not look up ... She mustn't look across at that other box. She mustn't even think.

Fiercely, she concentrated on the stage. The sets

were marvellous, the costumes beautiful. It looked like being an excellent production ...

She swallowed and let her eyelids flutter upwards. How cool he was, how completely detached. And he looked so well satisfied—with himself and with life. How long, she wondered, had he been back in Malta? And how long—how long had Jackie ...?

She turned her head away again. Hot tears blurred her vision, and as they threatened to spill over on to her cheeks she opened her evening bag and took out a handkerchief. Nobody must know. Nobody must even begin to guess what she felt.

But although she didn't realise it Peter had already seen everything ... the arrival of de Säez with his attractive companion, Susanna's reaction—even the surreptitious manoeuvres with the handkerchief. And his whole soul seemed to ache with anger and resentment and sympathy.

Butterfly turned out to be an enchanting young Italian soprano with a rare quality of softness and purity in her voice, and no small acting ability. She carried the exacting role as if it were part of herself, moving from heights of ecstatic joy and confidence to depths of tragic despair with a passion and sensitivity that held the audience motionless, and the rest of the cast supported her with true Italian competence and enthusiasm.

But when the interval arrived the audience came to life *en masse*, and nearly everyone made a move in the direction of the bar. Peter saw to it that he and Susanna went too. As the lights went up she had seen Ramiro look straight across at her, and she knew that they would be certain to meet in the bar, but at the same time she realised that the meeting could not be avoided. It had to happen some time.

The bar was modern and plain, and it was packed. Hardly anyone had room to turn round, and the roar of voices was deafening, but Peter managed to establish her in a reasonably quiet corner, and when he came back at last with the lemonade she had asked for he did his best to make audible conversation. More than five minutes went by and still there was no sign of Ramiro and his companion. And then, suddenly, they were there ... Ramiro carving his way expertly through the crowd, heading straight towards her. Jackie was just behind him, and as the four of them met Susanna noticed with detachment that she looked a little bewildered.

'Miss Baird—how delightful to see you!' But his eyes rested on her for barely a second before moving on to concentrate on the man beside her. Dully, she took in the fact that it seemed their relationship was now to be conducted as formally as possible. 'And Mr Hamblyn! It's very fortunate that we should all be here this evening—I returned from Sicily only last night, and have not yet had time to make my way up to Casa de Säez.' He glanced again at Susanna. 'Your grandfather is well, I hope? I look forward very much to discussing the progress of his book.'

'He's very well, thank you.' It surprised her that her voice could sound so composed and even. 'As a matter of fact, the first draft of the book is almost finished.' She added coolly: 'We've taken advantage of your hospitality quite long enough, but it won't be for very much longer. Grandpapa is tremendously appreciative of—of your help, but he always finishes his work in London.' It was true, and for a long time she had been hoping devoutly that the moment would soon arrive when he would be willing to go.

'Ah, does he? I am sorry to hear that, but I hope his departure will be delayed for some time yet. I shall not myself be spending much time at Casa de Säez—not for a few weeks, anyway—but I am happy in the thought that my house has been of use to Mr Debenham.'

It struck her that both his face and his voice seemed entirely devoid of expression, but that his accent was a little stronger than usual. He turned suddenly to Jackie Wilverton, and placed a hand—rather possessively, Susanna thought—beneath the Australian girl's arm.

'Forgive me—you know Miss Wilverton, I think. She has been on a short tour of the Middle East, but has paid Malta the compliment of returning for a while.'

Jackie opened her mouth as if to speak, but changed her mind and contented herself with directing a sparkling smile at her escort. She really was attractive, Susanna thought.

The first bell sounded, and a good many people started to move towards the doors leading back into the auditorium. The Marquis de Säez looked at Peter Hamblyn.

'I'm planning a large party,' he said suddenly, 'it will be held at Casa de Säez, early next week. You'll be receiving an invitation—I hope to see you there.' And before Peter could reply he turned back to Susanna. 'It may amuse you ... coloured lights, and dancing, and all the things that are supposed to appeal to young women of your age. Of course,'—was it her imagination, or did his voice soften slightly?—'Jackie will be there.'

Susanna didn't take in exactly what was said after that, but she did know that soon afterwards Peter took her arm, and the two couples separated. They returned to their respective boxes, the lights went down and the curtain rose again.

Afterwards, when she thought of that night at the Manoel Theatre, it seemed to her to have all the qualities of a feverish nightmare. The forlornness and ultimate torment of the unfortunate Madam Butterfly was one with her own misery, Puccini's music an expression of all the anguish and all the misplaced hope the world had ever known. And when the opera's tragic climax had finally been reached, and the stars were taking their curtain calls amid a storm of approbation, she felt all the cold bitterness of a return to reality. The beauty and the grandeur which art bestows on tragic love had gone with the fall of the curtain—and she was left with the dreary consciousness of a pain which would haunt her while she lived.

On the way back she tried to make conversation, but it was a miserable failure. Peter himself said very little, and she was grateful for the fact that he obviously understood and was trying to be as tactful as possible. But when, finally, they drew near to the gates of the Casa de Säez he spoke as if he could keep silent no longer.

'Listen, Susanna ...' His voice seemed to grate. 'I

don't know what there is or has been between you and de Säez, but believe me, judging from what I saw tonight, he's a swine!'

She said nothing, and they drove up to the door of the house in silence. Seeing the strain in her eyes, he turned down her rather feeble offer of coffee and said goodnight to her on the doorstep. Her hand felt cold as it lay in his, and he gave it a comforting squeeze.

'I know what's in your mind, and I know how you must feel about staying in his house. But stick it out a little while longer. Be at this party of his, let him see—let him think you couldn't care less.' He dropped her hand and smiled down at her. 'I won't be accepting his invitation, but I'll be thinking of you. And perhaps one day ...'

Afterwards she could never remember how she answered him. But at last, to her relief, he was gone, and she was free to creep up the silent stairs to her bedroom, and to lie in miserable wakefulness through what remained of the summer night.

A week went by, and during that time the Marquis spoke several times, by telephone, to Robert Debenham, but stayed well away from the Casa de Säez. Susanna knew that Carmen, also, was contacted, and that the maid received varied and detailed instructions in connection with the projected party. But she herself felt isolated and alone, and the nightmare quality of her life intensified. What was she waiting for—why couldn't she tell her grandfather that she had to get away? There was a limit to human endurance, and she knew that she had all but reached it. It was fantastic that she should still be staying in Ramiro's house, exposing herself daily to every kind of hurt ... unbelievable that she was going to attend his party. Whether he had any idea what she was going through she couldn't begin to guess, and she didn't want to. As for Jackie Wilverton ... did she constitute an 'interlude', or was she something more serious? Had a pretty face from Sydney at last unseated the memory of Célèstine? She didn't know, but she supposed that time would tell her.

On the morning of the party Emmanuel decorated the terrace and gardens with hundreds of coloured lights, and some of the more cumbersome furniture was moved from the *salotto* in order to make room for large numbers of guests. It was evidently expected that there would be dancing on the terrace, and in the corner of the dining-room, discreetly hidden by an antique Chinese screen, stereo equipment was fitted up. A catering firm was taking care of the buffet supper—something which would have been physically beyond the resources of Carmen—and late in the afternoon the head of the firm arrived with a van full of crates and boxes. Shortly afterwards his assistants arrived in a large white mini-bus, and the lower regions of the house began to be filled with noise and confusion.

Soon after six o'clock Susanna slipped downstairs, and out through the side door into the walled garden. That day, for the first time, temperatures had reached the hundred mark, and all over the house powerful electric fans had hummed steadily since early morning. The heat had seemed tangible and suffocating, and there had been no escape from it.

Now, as she emerged into the garden, it was still very

163

warm, but the worst was over for another day. The evening air soothed her, and so did the song of a sparrow in the smallest orange tree and the tinkle of the little fountain. She would have had Minu with her, but he was studying late with Brother Bernard ... and, for once, it was soothing to be alone. She wandered for nearly half an hour in the shadow of the trees, and then for ten minutes more she sat on the edge of the pool. At last, she got up and moved back towards the house. Before changing for the evening she went to see her grandfather.

In the hall she passed Brother Bernard, who was just leaving, and he smiled at her cordially. She had always got on well with the little friar, and if his reflections on the importance of stepmothers were still inclined to hurt her whenever she thought about them, she nevertheless appreciated his concern for Minu. She started to climb the stairs, stepping carefully around an enormous tray of wine-glasses which had been left a little way up—and then, from the other end of the hall, a voice called to her.

'Susanna!'

She turned, looking down, and saw that the Marquis was standing outside the door of his study. He was already in evening dress, and it was he who had spoken.

She hesitated, watching him uncertainly, and he came forward a few paces.

'Susanna, I want to talk to you.'

They were both motionless for several seconds, and then, as if drawn by a magnet, she moved down the stairs towards him. He held the door for her to precede him into his study, and when she was standing uneasily by his big Hepplewhite writing-table he pushed a chair towards her.

'Sit down. This conversation is not going to be easy for either of us, and you look as if the heat has almost knocked you out already.' He passed a hand across his own forehead. 'We'd better have some more air in here.'

One of the long windows was already open to the sweetness of the evening, but the other was still tightly shuttered and he flung it wide with a gesture of controlled irritation and impatience. Then he turned to stare hard at Susanna.

'You don't look well,' he commented, almost roughly. 'I thought you were used to hot climates.'

'I am.'

He shrugged. 'Then it's some other reason. Susanna, how old are you?'

'Twenty-three,' she told him quietly.

'Then you're old enough to have discovered before this that "falling in love" does not pay. It's a crime against oneself.'

Susanna turned pale. She wanted to say something, but nothing would come. Instead, she bit her lip so hard that she winced.

He began to pace up and down, pausing every now and then to look at her with eyes as dark and hard as pieces of ebony. At last he stopped, placed both hands squarely on the surface of the big desk, and stood staring down at his own strong fingers.

'I should not be talking to you like this ... that is what most people would say. Convention demands that I blandly assume you are now indifferent to me ...

that I "forget" everything that has happened between us.' He raised his eyes so that he could look straight into her face, and for the first time she noticed the tautness about his mouth. He took a deep breath and straightened up. 'I will not insult you,' he said slowly, 'with that sort of lie.'

She swallowed. The breath seemed suspended in her throat.

'I know you love me—and I know you're suffering for it. But, believe me, if we married—if we did anything to encourage that love—you would suffer more.' His voice became harsh and rasping, and the words came jerkily. 'Love has to be killed ... driven from one's mind, dug out of one's soul. Never, never link your life with the life of someone you love—as far as possible, never love at all!' He paused, breathing heavily. 'I know. I married a woman I adored. She was young and very beautiful, and I thought she felt the same about me—perhaps she did. But four years after our marriage she became bored and ran away to New York with a Swedish film director whom she had met here in Malta ... here in this house.'

Susanna gave a startled gasp of sympathy. He turned away from her.

'She took Minu with her—he was two years old. As their plane was coming in to land at Kennedy Airport something went wrong with the undercarriage, and there was nothing that could be done about it. They crashed in flames. Célèstine was killed instantly, and so was the man. Minu ... Minu was only injured—his foot was caught in the wreckage. The rescue workers could not understand it.'

'I'm sorry,' she whispered.

He looked at her oddly. 'Don't be. Don't waste your life being sorry. There is tragedy everywhere in the world, wherever you look, wherever you turn. Look past it, and be happy.' He walked to one of the windows, and stood gazing out at the dusty green of the tired fir trees. On the desk between them an electric fan hummed monotonously. When he spoke again his voice was harsher than she had ever heard it. 'Be happy, Susanna, and go away from me. Go away from me, because I love you ... more, much more than I ever loved Célèstine.'

Susanna's head began to swim, and every pulse in her body throbbed. She wondered if her ears were playing tricks on her.

'What did you say?' she asked.

He swung round angrily. 'I told you I loved you. It happens to be the truth. And it's also the reason why, tonight, I shall ask Jackie Wilverton to marry me!'

She looked at him. Her face was shocked. 'If—if you love me,' she said slowly, faintly, 'why——'

'I've told you why! Because I love you and you love me, and we would hurt and destroy one another. It would not even be swift, humane destruction! We would stab each other with a thousand knives before finally administering the *coup de grâce*.' His eyes narrowed and his face grew lean and angular. 'I want to avoid that fate—this time I would not recover—and I want to avoid it for you, too. Unfortunately I shall have to marry, for it has become obvious to me that Minu needs a stepmother. A Maltese girl of my own kind might expect too much, but Jackie will expect nothing but the position I can give her. She is a nice girl and she will do very well, but she's not in love with me and never will be, just as I will never be in love with her. As far as I am concerned that makes our marriage possible.'

He moved back to the desk, and stood looking down at the papers scattered about its gleaming surface. In an odd, controlled tone, he said: 'I would advise you to marry also. Pick someone pleasant ... someone you like. Someone like Peter Hamblyn.'

Susanna felt as if she were going to choke. The stifling atmosphere of the warm evening seemed to be closing in on her, and the small, sombrely furnished room was like a prison. She stood up, feeling her legs quiver beneath her.

'I hope ... you'll be happy,' she said with difficulty. 'I hope everything turns out really well!'

And then she headed blindly for the door. Ramiro St Vincent de Säez made no attempt to stop her.

CHAPTER TWELVE

SUSANNA lay on her bed. It was almost morning. Below her window, in the garden, a woman was laughing. There was a man's voice, too, and it sounded coaxing, teasing. It sounded as if the party had been fairly satisfactory from their point of view.

Tired of staring at the dimly visible ceiling, she turned on her side. After a brief silence the amplified voice of the record-player came to life again, and a male singer started to croon rhythmically. *'Oh, Spanish eyes ...'*

She wished he would be quiet. She wished they would all be quiet. They had been dancing and laughing and clinking champagne glasses all through the long, hot airless night, and there must come a time when it would end ... when the music would stop and they would all go away, taking their happiness with them. *'A silence fell with the waking bird, and a hush with the setting moon ...'* she thought. Tennyson again. She wished her head would stop revolving in circles, and also that it would stop aching.

Somewhere down below there was a sound of shattering glass, followed by a high-pitched giggle. Hoping at least to still the throbbing in her head, Susanna slipped off the bed and went to lean out of the window. Immediately below her two dark-haired girls with all-revealing necklines were evidently trying to thwart the efforts of a thin, bespectacled young man to anoint them with champagne, and judging by their high-pitched, excited squeals they had already consumed more than enough of the beverage in question.

'Anton, no!' shrieked one of the girls in English— Susanna had made the discovery that most of the Maltese aristocracy spoke English among themselves, at least part of the time. The other girl giggled again, and Anton said something she didn't catch. Then they disappeared round the side of the house, and the walled garden was temporarily empty again.

Susanna turned back into the room. It had been a very long night, for it had begun soon after seven o'clock in the evening. She had left Ramiro and come straight upstairs to her room, and there she had remained, alone. Once Carmen had been sent to find out what had happened to her, but she had pleaded the excuse of a shattering migraine headache. Carmen had offered her aspirins and hot drinks, had looked horrified at the thought that the Signurina would be missing all the fun and had wanted to do more to make her comfortable. But even she had eventually been persuaded to leave, and ever since then Susanna had been left in blessed isolation.

She dropped back on to the bed, and had just resumed her study of the ceiling when there came a light, muffled knock on the door. At first she wasn't certain it was a knock, but when it was repeated she sat up, pushing the hair out of her eyes, and called 'Come in.'

The door slowly opened, and Carmen appeared. She was looking very smart in her starched white cap and frilly apron, but she was also beginning to look exhausted ... and something else.

'Signurina——' Her eyes were wide and scared. 'It's Minu. I thought he would be here.'

'Why?' For some reason Susanna felt uneasy. 'Can't you find him?' She slid her feet to the floor and stood up at once.

'He is not in his bedroom, signurina. He is not in the house, anywhere. Now Emmanuel looks in the garden.' She clasped her hands fearfully over her apron. 'Minu never do like this before.'

The need for action had shaken Susanna out of herself, and she was instantly clear-headed. Switching on her bedside light, she went straight to the long line of hanging cupboards and took out a dress.

'Don't worry, Carmen, we'll find him. He can't have gone far. He's probably hiding somewhere, watching people and listening to the music.'

But Minu wasn't anywhere to be found, and half an hour later Emmanuel sought out the Marquis and gave him the news that his son seemed to have disappeared. Susanna was still helping to search the gardens at the time, and when she returned he had already left the house. He had set out to organise the men of the district into a search party which would cover the surrounding countryside, and to her relief she didn't have to see him.

None of the guests had been told anything about the disappearance of Minu, and out on the terrace some of them were still dancing. Although it was now well past five o'clock there were as many expensive-looking cars jamming the drive and forecourt as there had been at midnight, and several times in the course of the search Susanna found herself forced to squeeze a way between them. It didn't look as if many of those who had been invited could have failed to turn up.

She had seen nothing of Jackie Wilverton, and it occurred to her to wonder whether the engagement had been announced.

The eastern sky was paling with the first grey light of dawn when at last she allowed herself to be persuaded that there was nothing more to be done for the time being. Her grandfather, she was told, had gone to bed some hours before, and so after a few more words with a distraught and tearful Carmen she went back upstairs to her own room. Once there, she sat by the window in the cool, misty dawn, watching the daylight grow and wondering about Minu.

Where could he have got to—small and lame as he was? What was he doing? And, above all, why was he doing it?

After a time she began to hear a revving of engines, and it became clear that the guests had started to leave. Voices and a good deal of laughter came wafting round from the front of the house, and car doors banged. A short time later nearly everybody seemed to have gone, and one part of her mind wondered again, in a detached sort of way, about Jackie Wilverton. Presumably she was still somewhere in the building, but where?

Probably, she decided, waiting in Ramiro's study.

Slowly an hour crept by, and then another hour. The house was silent and still with the tranquillity of early morning, and several times she almost slept. The sun rose, flooding everything with warm golden light, and below her window the garden shimmered.

And then she heard the sound of footsteps outside her door, and there was a quick, urgent rapping. Without waiting for a response, Carmen opened the door and came inside.

'Signurina, I think we hear news!'

Susanna jumped to her feet. 'What is it—have they found him?'

'No, no, not they found him. But maybe someone see him.'

'Where, Carmen? How long ago?'

'I think one hour. Is-Signur and the others not come back, so I telephone to the police. Is-Signur said if he is not back by six o'clock, I must telephone.'

'Yes ... well, what did they say?'

'They said they will keep watching for him. Then, just now, they telephone here. They say Minu has gone to Gozo.'

'To Gozo?' Susanna stared at the other woman. 'But how could—what makes them think so?'

'Someone see him on the ferry-boat. A little boy just like Minu, all alone.'

'Well, couldn't they stop him at the other end—I mean, when the boat reached Gozo?'

Carmen spread her hands. 'No, no, too late.'

'Then he's in Gozo now?'

'I think ... but maybe it's not him.'

'Well, if it is someone will have to go after him. You say nobody has come back yet—from the search?'

'Not yet.' An anxious shrug. 'I think maybe they go a long way.'

Susanna thought rapidly, and came to a decision. 'Then I'll go after him. Carmen, do you know where I can find the Lotus—and the keys?'

Carmen nodded. 'Yes, I bring them to you. But, signurina—you go to Gozo before?'

'No, but that doesn't matter. I can find my way to the ferry, and that's the main thing.'

'But maybe they won't let you take the car. In summer you need to book ... two, three days before.'

'Well, there's always a chance, isn't there? But if I can't get the car on board I'll leave it over here. I could give the keys to the police, or something.'

Twenty minutes later she was setting off down the drive at the wheel of the Lotus. When Ramiro got back from the search he might be annoyed, but she didn't really see why he should be—and in any case it didn't matter what Ramiro thought of anything she did. The important thing was that somebody ought to catch up with Minu as quickly as possible, particularly if he really were in Gozo. And if it should turn out to be a false alarm it wouldn't matter too much, because Ramiro would still be directing operations in Malta.

It wasn't long before she reached the brow of the hill that overlooked the landing-stage. Below her lay the wide curve of the Mediterranean, calm as a mill-pond and intensely blue. And beyond, looming through the last of the mist like some legendary fairy-tale country, she glimpsed the softly smudged outlines of Gozo.

Braking gently, she let the Lotus run slowly down the hill towards the tiny, unpretentious harbour. Besides a wide stone jetty there was nothing to be seen but a shuttered café, a weatherbeaten police station and a short column of motor vehicles that were evidently queueing up for the privilege of being allowed on board the next ferryboat. There were several private cars in the queue, a furniture van and a lorry loaded with Coca-Cola. Falling in behind them, she switched off the Lotus's engine and sat back to wait.

It was already hot, and there seemed to be very little breeze from the motionless, glittering sea. There was nothing whatsoever to indicate at what time the next ferry was expected, and she supposed the only thing she could do was hope for the best. She had been told that the boats crossed in a more or less continuous shuttle service during the summer months, and it surely wouldn't be too long before one of them put in an appearance. In any case there was no real point in asking anyone, for she had come determined to wait as long as might be necessary.

But as it turned out it wasn't very long before one of the broad, green-and-white steamers began to come into view, and although at first the steamer was only a dot on the surface of the sea, she approached very fast. Despite her clumsy car-ferry shape she manoeuvred quite gracefully in the water, and Susanna was impressed by the speed and ease with which she suddenly came about and swung alongside the jetty. Men who had been waiting on the quayside rushed forward to tie her up, and within minutes a yawning opening had appeared in her bows. A ramp was lowered and cars began to crawl ashore, while from the decks above hundreds of foot-passengers swarmed down to disembark.

By this time, Susanna noticed, the queue of cars behind her had grown to such an extent that it stretched out of sight around a bend, and she felt a twinge of uneasiness. The rule was that all booked vehicles boarded the steamer first—Carmen had told her that. If, after they were aboard, there was still room the others were taken one by one from the queue. But there might turn out to be space for only two or three of them—and sometimes, according to Carmen, no unbooked cars could be accommodated. After a time a man came along the line, checking, and Susanna was told that like all the other drivers who had been lacking in forethought she must wait. Perhaps there would be room ... and perhaps there wouldn't. Keeping her fingers crossed, she waited.

The ferryboat, the S.S. *Melitaland*, was large and very roomy, with space in her cavernous depths for ninety average-sized cars, but her capacity was obviously being stretched to the limit, and Susanna, watching, began to wonder how she managed to keep afloat. Before the first car was allowed to move several heavy lorries and a milk float had disappeared into the bowels of the steamer, and as they were manoeuvred into position she seemed to shudder. But after that she swallowed up car after car, and ten minutes later all the booked vehicles had been taken aboard. One by one, very slowly, the others began to be beckoned forward, and at last it came to Susanna's turn. She held her breath while the car that had been in front of her was carefully fitted into position, but even after that there was still room, and, smiling, the policeman on duty waved her on. Having bought her ticket she allowed herself to be guided, half pushed into a postage-stamp space between two Minis—and then, with a sigh of relief, she left the Lotus and went up on deck.

There were hundreds of people on board, some tourists, some locals, and most of them were obviously out to enjoy themselves. When, a few minutes later, the engines came to life a raucous cheer went up, and then a group of young Maltese began to sing in harmony. The *Melitaland* gathered speed, and the harbour fell away behind them.

Susanna leant against the rail. She felt sick with reaction, and the glare of the dancing blue water all around was making her head ache. Where was she going? What on earth was she doing? She supposed she was going to find Minu—that at least made sense

—and she must just try and keep that goal in front of her. Nothing else mattered ... there was nothing else *to* matter. She clung to the rail as if it were a lifeline, almost afraid to turn round. Behind and all around her there were people with happy faces, and she didn't want to look at them. Perhaps that was childish, and perhaps it wasn't. She didn't know; she didn't know anything—except that for her, on this lovely summer morning, life was an empty thing.

Twenty minutes later they reached the long break-water guarding Gozo's only port and several tourists rushed to the rails to take photographs. The little harbour was colourful and crowded with boats, and it had a lively, businesslike air about it. Above and behind the ground climbed steeply, and the straggling village of Mgarr climbed with it. At the very top of the hill there was poised a church with a spire—the first Susanna had seen in the Maltese Islands—and as a deep, melodious clangour of bells drifted out across the sunny water she remembered it was Sunday morning.

Rather uncertainly, she drove ashore—and then stopped, wondering what she ought to do next. The first thing, she supposed, would be to get in touch with the local police, and seeing a police station on the quay she left the car and went inside. The officer to whom she spoke knew all about the case, but he could only report that nobody had seen Minu disembark. Undoubtedly the boy must be somewhere on Gozo, and of course he would be found, but ... well, if the signurina liked to drive into Victoria, the capital of the island, she might be able to find something out for herself. Victoria—or Rabat, as the local people called it—was only three miles away, and a child could easily have gone there by bus. Naturally inquiries were being made, but ...

Susanna thanked him, and went outside again into the blistering heat. A signpost showed her the way to Victoria, and she drove up a long hill leading out of Mgarr. Dimly, she began to recognise the fact that Gozo was a beautiful island, a place of little green hills and romantic, honey-coloured villages, of donkey-carts and winding roads and brooding, sunlit peace. In the cottage doorways old women in black who on any other day would have been making lace sat relaxing in the sun, and everywhere there were pretty dark-eyed children who stopped to stare at every car that passed.

In Victoria—which turned out to be a peaceful little town gathered around an ancient walled fortress—she parked the car near the central square, and set out to make inquiries. She went into shops, cafés, hotels, and finally the well-organised bus station, but nobody had seen a little boy with any sort of a limp. Everywhere people were kind and concerned, and some had suggestions to make—had she tried the restaurant across the road, the sweet-shop six doors away ... the police? But nowhere was there any trace of Minu, and, after a time, she began to wonder whether her trip to Gozo had after all been nothing but a wild goose chase. Dejectedly, she went back inside the principal hotel and asked whether she could use the telephone.

When she got through to the Casa de Säez Carmen answered, and Susanna learned that the Marquis, having completed a fruitless search of the surrounding countryside, had set out again to follow up another possibility. Somebody at the southern end of the Island thought they had seen a lame boy, but—well, it didn't sound like Minu. Carmen's voice shook, and she broke off.

Susanna told her as confidently as she could that she still hoped to find Minu in Gozo, left a message for her grandfather—who was evidently still in bed—and hung up.

Ramiro hadn't left any sort of message for her. No doubt he was being supported by Jackie ...

Feeling tired and flat, she went into the hotel lounge and ordered a coffee. The waitress, a local girl, was cheerful and friendly, and as it was still too early to be very busy she wanted to talk. Susanna didn't see any point, this time, in going into details about Minu, and she simply answered the questions put to her. Yes, it was her first visit to Gozo. Yes ... it was a lovely island. She sipped her coffee. The girl lingered.

'Today it is a *festa*. Not here—in one of the villages. That is why Rabat is quiet.'

Susanna's attention was caught. 'A *festa*?'

'You would like to see it? Are you staying in Gozo tonight?'

'Perhaps, I don't know. Where is the *festa*?'

'In Nadur. It's our biggest village—I think two miles from here. But if you want to see the *festa*, you must go this evening, about six o'clock.'

Susanna finished her coffee. 'Thanks ... I might do that.' For a second she closed her eyes. If Minu hadn't been found by tonight ... well, it was just a chance. She paid for her coffee, said goodbye to the girl and went out into the hall. A friendly receptionist looked up at her approach. One single room? Well, yes, they could just do that. She was lucky ... if it had been the following night they would have been completely full.

She spent that afternoon cruising around the coastal villages, searching crowded beaches. The heat was scorching and her head ached. Gozo was only a tiny island—nine miles long and three miles wide—but it had a lot of beaches and tiny, sequestered coves, and at the height of a busy summer it was a confusing place in which to look for one small boy.

Towards five o'clock she returned to her hotel, limp and exhausted, and went upstairs to lie on her bed. There was a small electric fan in the room and she turned it on, but the air was suffocating, and her head swam.

Whenever she thought of Minu cold waves of anxiety broke over her. Where could he be ... what could he be doing? She had given Carmen the number of the hotel and had asked her, if there should be any news, to ring and leave a message. But there had been no message ... what was happening in Malta?

Unable to lie still, she got up off the bed and took a shower in the adjoining bathroom. Since she had no luggage of any sort with her she could not change her dress, but the shower refreshed her a little, and the slim white sun-dress in which she had started out that morning had somehow stayed presentable. She took a comb out of her bag and ran it through her hair, then washed her face and applied a little make-up. Her face, reflected in the dressing-table mirror, looked wan despite its light coating of tan, and her eyes were dark and haunted.

180

There was a telephone by the bed, and picking up the receiver she got herself put through once again to the Casa de Säez. Carmen answered, and this time she sounded tearful. There was no news ... nothing at all. Throughout the day there had been false alarms, and Is-Signur had dashed about the island following them up, but nothing had come of any of them. Bus and taxi drivers had been questioned, and so had children playing in the streets, but nobody had seen anything at all. The only thing to be thankful for was that all the hospitals had been checked, and there had been no report of any accident ... that, at least, was some source of comfort.

Susanna hung up. Once again there had been no message for her from Ramiro. Didn't he realise that she, too, was half out of her mind with anxiety? Didn't he care at all that she was alone on another island, straining every nerve to find his son? She hadn't even been able to speak to her grandfather, for he, apparently, was 'walking in the garden'. She had never felt so completely alone.

At about a quarter to six she closed the door of her room behind her, then went downstairs and out into the street. The sun was slowly sinking westwards and it was cooler. She climbed into the Lotus, which was parked beside the kerb, let in the clutch and moved away slowly down the wide main street. Irritatingly, the falling sun was in her eyes, but she had already studied a map and once outside the town she had no difficulty in finding the right turning.

For part of the way the road to Nadur was broad and straight, lined on either side by Governmentplanted oleander bushes, but after a while it began to climb, encircling a massive hill with a series of dramatic S-bends. The view on the left became spectacular, and at any other time she would have been fascinated by the beauty of the terraced hillsides and still-green valleys spread out below her. As it was, though, she kept her eyes firmly fixed on the road ahead.

Nadur, a huge, straggling village, was spread across the flat plateau at the top of the hill, and it was quite obviously *en fête*. As Susanna approached somebody in the heart of the village fired a petard, and it was followed by another, and then another. The little puffs of silvery-white smoke drifted slowly away over the rooftops like fragments of cotton wool, and more followed them. The organisers of the celebrations were warming up.

Cars seemed to be parked as much as a quarter of a mile beyond the limits of the village, and she soon decided that she had better find a place for the Lotus as quickly as possible. Then she could lock it up, leave it and join the huge crowd streaming towards the centre of Nadur. That way she would stand the best chance of seeing Minu—if he were anywhere to be seen.

The crowd was noisy, happy and colourful, and the further she went the denser it became. Apart from the great events of Christmas and Easter the annual *festa* is the highest point of the year for any Maltese or Gozitan village, and it was something evidently nobody wanted to miss. It was a time to forget problems and be happy, to laugh and chatter and relax. And for young, unattached men and women—or so Susanna

182

had heard—it was a time to meet new people, make new friends ... a time to fall in love.

The whole thing revolved, she knew, around a religious ritual, and it was for this reason that everybody was heading towards the great parish church in the centre of the village. At some time during the evening an image of Nadur's patron saint would be carried out of the church and borne in procession around the village, accompanied by a marching band and a crowd of eager, reverent spectators. Bells would ring, the band would play and the sky would blaze with fireworks.

And, she hoped desperately, somewhere in the crowd she would find Minu. She didn't know why she was so certain that he would somehow make his way to the *festa*, but she was.

Keeping her eyes open all the time, she allowed herself to be swept along by the human tide, and at last they reached Nadur's big main square. Here the crowd was dense, and it was difficult to move, or to see anything apart from the great church with its twin *campanili*, the tops of the oleander trees and the upper windows of the houses surrounding the square. Every window and every balcony was packed with spectators, and there was a sort of tense, breathless excitement in the air. Susanna tried to go on pushing her way through the dense, surging mass of people, but it was impossible, and she had to content herself with standing on tiptoe and watching all the time.

The image of the saint was due to make its appearance at seven o'clock, and now the moment had almost arrived. Slowly the seconds ticked away, and in the square there was an all-enveloping hush. Everyone's eyes were turned in one direction only ... some faces reflected a kind of ecstasy. And then, punctually at seven, the great doors of the church were flung wide, and the procession emerged. Simultaneously, fireworks exploded above the heads of the crowd, two bands struck up and all the bells began to peal as if the ringers' lives depended on the results of their efforts. The noise was shattering, but nobody showed any signs of recoiling from it. The jewelled and gilded image, supported by four bearers, began to move down the church steps, and as it passed into the thick of the crowd, attended by priests and monks and preceded by one of the bands, everybody began to clap. More fireworks soared into the luminous turquoise sky, and the ground shook.

Susanna felt slightly dazed. The crowd began to shift a little, some people moving off to follow the procession and the rest settling down to enjoy themselves. Under the oleander trees there were stalls selling nougat—the traditional *festa* delicacy—and there seemed to be dozens of bars. Now that it was possible to move again she set out to continue her search—glancing at every child, looking in every doorway, even stopping passers-by to ask if they had seen a small boy with a limp.

Two hours later she had made no progress, and it had begun to seem to her that she was living through a nightmare from which there would never be any escape. People were looking at her—some of the local boys stared embarrassingly, or it would have been embarrassing if she had had any feelings left. And now the procession was making its way back towards the church, and the crowd in the square was getting dense again. One thing was certain, Minu wasn't there, and almost certainly never had been.

Standing by a nougat stall, she watched the swaying image as it came back into view. Everyone was surging forward again, getting as close as possible to the gilded figure, and she realised that nothing could have been more genuine than their eager, passionate adoration. The band began to play *Ave Maria*, and almost at once the crowd took it up.

'*Ave, ave, ave Maria . . . !*'

They pressed forward towards the statue, one or two policeman good-humouredly holding them back. Looking around at a big, burly young countryman standing just beside her, Susanna saw that there were tears on his cheeks, and others, too, were weeping.

The procession went past, back into the church, and a large part of the crowd followed it inside. Standing in the lamplit square, under the distant stars, Susanna suddenly felt almost alone. She hadn't realised before how tired she was, but now weariness, anxiety and misery swept over her, overwhelming her defences. Beads of perspiration broke out on her forehead, and she felt herself sway slightly.

Then, behind her, a voice said: 'Susanna!'

CHAPTER THIRTEEN

RAMIRO's arm was around her, and it was very comforting. Hardly knowing what she was doing, she leant against him.

'My car is just around the corner.' His voice sounded calm, but oddly husky. 'The first thing we had better do is get you into it.'

Less than a minute later Susanna found herself being helped into the front passenger seat of the Jaguar, which was parked in a quiet, deserted alleyway, and when the door was securely closed upon her Ramiro walked round in front of the bonnet and got in beside her. The feeling of comfort evaporated, and memory flooded back. She started to cry ... dry, tearing sobs of exhaustion.

'Minu—I couldn't find him. I ...'

'Minu is safe. Fast asleep, by now, in my hotel.'

'S-safe?' Slowly she looked round at him. 'Are you sure?'

'Quite sure. As soon as I heard, early this morning, that you had gone to Gozo after hearing that police report, I knew you were right. Minu had often talked about wanting to come over here, and it seemed likely that if he were going to run away he would run away to Gozo. I stayed for a few hours, checking on various other reports, but I had made up my mind that if you had not found him by this afternoon I was coming over here to join you. I arrived on one of the last ferries, and at about seven o'clock I found him—trying to hitch a lift. He was coming up here.'

'I—I thought he would. That's why I came up here. But I didn't find him, and ...'

She began to cry again. All the time she could feel his eyes on her—boring into her. At last, through stiff lips, she said:

'Where is Jackie—Jackie Wilverton?'

There was a short silence, and when he spoke there was a faint quiver of amusement in his voice.

'How should I know? Planning her next world trip, probably.'

'But you're going to marry her.'

'Heaven protect me! Listen, Susanna ...' She had never heard his voice so caressing, and, startled, she stopped crying. 'I am going to get married, but not to Jackie Wilverton.'

Like a bewildered child, she persisted. 'But—but you said ...' Her voice broke.

'I know.' Suddenly his hand came out and touched her hair. 'Susanna, look at me.'

Reluctantly, she obeyed ... and then as their eyes met something seemed to turn over inside her. The next moment his arms were around her, and he was holding her with a passionate tenderness she had never experienced before.

'Forgive me,' he murmured. 'Darling, forgive me. Ever since you left me last night I've known how dreadfully wrong I was. I couldn't live without you, you're the centre of my life. I've been in agony for the last few weeks, just trying to exist away from you. Célèstine was a charming doll who fascinated me, but I never felt for her what I feel for you. You haven't—changed your mind, have you?'

Dazed, floating on a silver cloud, hardly daring to believe in the reality of what was happening, she clung to him. Against his shoulder, she whispered:

'I could never change my mind. I love you more than anything in the world, and—and that will always be the same, whether you want me or not. But ... but that night in Mdina——'

'Don't remind me.' His voice was suddenly almost grim, and his hold on her tightened. 'Susanna, you know I didn't mean it? That talk about an amusing interlude—you'll never understand quite how it's haunted me. But I didn't know what I was doing. We were falling so deeply in love, and all I could think was that something had to be done to stop it, for your sake as well as mine. Now I know better. I know it's going to be all right—for both of us.'

She looked up at him with the last traces of uncertainty in her eyes.

'And you—you really want me?'

'I want you.'

He bent his head, and their lips met. Light-headed with wonder and ecstasy, she felt as if the whole world were touched with stardust.

Some time later he smiled down at her a little wryly.

'Minu has certainly never had any doubts about the stepmother he wants. Do you know that he ran away last night because he had been listening outside the study window when I announced that I was going to marry the Wilverton girl? I didn't know it when I made up my mind that I couldn't face life without you, but he seems to have felt the same. Apparently he just made his way down the drive and kept on going until he reached the main road. Then he got himself a lift to Marfa. He told the driver of the car—who must have been rather gullible—that he had got lost in the course of a Sunday afternoon outing, but that his parents would be meeting him at the harbour!'

188

Her heart contracted. 'Poor Minu! Is he really all right?'

'Very much so. He's quite tough, you know. And he'll be tougher when we've taken him to London for a straightening operation on his ankle.' She looked up at him inquiringly, and he smiled at her. 'I know how strongly you've always felt about that, and I've made all the arrangements. Later on he'll be going to school in England, too. I should have done all these things a long time ago, but I was so sunk in bitterness and self-pity that I didn't even think of it. Your grandfather had something to say about that this afternoon.'

'Grandpapa?' She was startled.

'Yes. I was telling him that I was determined to marry you, and he remarked that it was a pity I hadn't snapped out of my "self-absorption" sooner. He is the sort of person it's useful to have in any family.' He smiled. 'And it looks as if we may be going to have him in the family twice over. He seems to have become quite attached to my Aunt Marthese, and since he is certainly going to need a replacement for you ...'

Susanna laughed softly, happily. 'I like your Aunt Marthese. I'll have to teach her how to stand up to him.'

Possessively, he gathered her back into his arms. 'Never mind Aunt Marthese. Tell me how much you love me.'

She told him, her lips against his cheek.

Harlequin Reader Service
ORDER FORM

Mail coupon to:
Harlequin Reader Service,
M.P.O. Box 707,
Niagara Falls, New York 14302

Canadian Residents send to:
Harlequin Reader Service,
Stratford, Ont. N5A 6W4

Please send me by return mail the books that I have checked.
I am enclosing 95¢ for each book ordered.

Please check volumes requested:

☐ 1	☐ 11	☐ 20	☐ 29
☐ 2	☐ 12	☐ 21	☐ 30
☐ 3	☐ 13	☐ 22	☐ 31
☐ 4	☐ 14	☐ 23	☐ 32
☐ 5	☐ 15	☐ 24	☐ 33
☐ 7	☐ 16	☐ 25	☐ 34
☐ 8	☐ 17	☐ 26	☐ 35
☐ 9	☐ 18	☐ 27	☐ 36
☐ 10	☐ 19	☐ 28	☐ 37

Number of books ordered_____ @ 95¢ each = $_____

Postage and handling = $_____.25

TOTAL = $_____

NAME _____
(please print)

ADDRESS _____

CITY _____

STATE/PROV. _____ ZIP/POSTAL CODE _____

Offer expires December 31, 1977   ROM 2067

Send for your copy today!

The Harlequin Romance Catalog FREE!

Here's your chance to catch up on all the wonderful Harlequin Romance novels you may have missed because the books are no longer available at your favorite booksellers.

Complete the coupon and mail it to us. By return mail, we'll send you a copy of the latest Harlequin catalog. Then you'll be able to order the books you want directly from us.

Clip and mail coupon today.